This Way Out

This Way Out

by
Frederic Isham

Edited by Hannah Downs

Whitlock Publishing
Alfred, New York

This Way Out by Frederic Isham

Originally Published by Bobbs Merill Company, Indianapolis, Indiana. 1917.

This edition published by Whitlock Publishing, Alfred, New York. 2018. www.whitlockpublishing.com

Editorial matter © Hannah Downs

Cover design by Hannah Downs.

Cover art from English Heritage.

ISBN: 978-1-943115-17-4

ACKNOWLEDGEMENTS

Thank you Dr. Grove for all of your help and expertise.

The early twentieth century in America was a time of great social change. From the acquisition of the Panama Canal in 1904 to United States entering World War I in 1917, and all the social and political changes that went on in between, America was quickly strengthening its national identity. Many writers took to their work to critique their society, and some began to call for changes in the way women were treated, and the expectations placed on them both in and out of the home. One of those writers was Frederic S. Isham, who chose to call attention to the changing domestic sphere and the roles of women in and outside of it. His novel *This Way Out* makes exactly this kind of social criticism.

Frederic Stewart Isham was born in Detroit, Michigan in 1865, and while not much is known about his early schooling, it is assumed that this is where his education took place. In 1895, he married Helen Frue and moved to New York City to further his writing. There, he published the novels *A Man and His Money* (1912), *Under the Rose* (1903), *The Nutcracker*, *The Strollers* (1902), *Nothing but The Truth* (1914), *Black Friday* (1904), *The Social Bucaneer* (1910), *Aladdin from Broadway* (1913), and *The Lady of the Mount* (1908). All of Frederic Isham's novels contain an element of social criticism as they focus on gender, class roles, and American society. Later, some of his works were even produced on Broadway, such as *Jack and Jill* in 1923. *3 Live Ghosts*, his only comedy, was made into an Alfred Hitchcock film in 1922. These adaptations were produced posthumously as Isham died in 1922, but he was still given writer's credit for them. Even though not much is known about this author, his books have made a large impact on the literary world.

In his many novels, Isham wrote about and critiqued society, often focusing on women and their relationship to the domestic sphere. Other writers of the time such as the popular realist authors Henry James and Edith Wharton also made critiques centered on gender roles in America. James used his gothic novella *The Turn of the Screw* to comment on the role of the governess in the domestic sphere, and the impact of that role on women's mental health. In Wharton's *Ethan Frome*, the expectations of women in the elite upper class are brought to light, which contemporary scholars often compared to Wharton's own unhappy marriage. Like both of these writers, Isham uses his novel to explore American society in the early 1900s. Isham critiqued the way women were treated by their society and questioned the expectations placed on them. For example, his main character does not rely on any man physically, but she still yearns for a connection that she finds with her servant. Isham uses his characters to critique the limited and restrictive roles of women in society. In *This Way Out*, Isham uses the wealthy Lady Langlenshire to show how an elitist upper class woman treats her Greek domestic help, Alexander. Henrik Ibsen's *A Doll House* explores similar themes as the main character struggles to find out who she is, who she is not, and who her father and husband have created her to be. All of these works reveal that the role of a woman in the house is a problematic social construct.

Frederic Isham could also be considered to be ahead of his time as his works about gender roles came before women procured their right to vote in 1920. Before the early 1900s, laws greatly restricted a woman's ability to own property. One of these laws, passed in 1839, stated that women could not own property without the approval of their husbands. And in 1875, the Supreme Court ruled that women are in a "special category of non-voting citizens." It was not until 1900 that married women were allowed complete control over their possessions and earnings. Isham's novel explores these rapidly changing roles for women by having Lady Langlenshire in charge of her own being completely. She has her wealth and controls her own daily life. By having a character who was challenging long-held social expectations, Isham shows his disagreement with those expectations. His novels reveal that he believes that things should be much different than they are.

Another theme present in *This Way Out* is that of a woman's role in the house. In the early 1900s when this novel was published, women were typically expected to have babies and oversee the daily goings-on in the domestic sphere. They were not supposed to have an opinion on anything outside the house and certainly shouldn't be involved in any way with government and politics, and they were expected to have little to no control over the family's financials. These tasks, and being in charge of the women, fell to the fathers and husbands of families. At this time, women were not allowed to vote, and were thus strongly discouraged from any participation in the politics and business around them. However, Isham's main character makes a radical departure from social expectations. Lady Langlenshire is a wealthy woman of the upper class who answers to no man. Many of the other women in her society are the property of their husbands or fathers, and they do not have the daily control over what they do in their own lives. A wealthy lady such as herself would have her finances controlled by her husband or father, and her only worry would be overseeing the servants who worked in the household. Even though it is expected that Lady Langlenshire marry, she is in no hurry to find a husband who would eventually take her wealth and the control her property. She is in charge of her own money, travel, and lifestyle. And, central to the main plot of the novel, she is in charge of her manservant, and that control gives her a type of agency.

This Way Out also explores the role of domestic help in the United States. Ever since the founding of America, there has always been domestic help. It has changed and evolved over the decades, but it has always been there. Domestic helpers have had duties such as child-care, cooking, cleaning, and other general housework. Domestic helpers were members of the lower class, and often immigrants. They were typically desperate for work and would do whatever they could to support themselves and their families. As a result, they were often treated as inferiors by their employers. In *This Way Out*, Lady Langlenshire makes it her personal mission to "fix" her servant, Alexander. Her attitude was common among members of the upper class towards their lower-class servants. Lady Langlenshire wants to change everything about Alexander, from his posture to the way he speaks. She feels that it is her job to "better" him. Alexander is a Greek immigrant who has very broken English, so he often does not mind the help and does not fight it. He does not appreciate the nitpicking, but because of his status as a servant, he is in no position to voice such complaints.

Many European citizens, much like Alexander, often immigrated to the United States in hopes of a better life for themselves and their families. But more often than not, this is far from what they found. Many decided to leave their homelands because they wanted a safer and more secure life than what could be found in their own countries. However, many immigrants were forced to live in unsanitary conditions and had to work jobs that were difficult and dangerous. This was due to the many immigration laws that made life for would-be United States citizens challenging. Many immigrants found themselves working in the homes of America's wealthy for very low wages that they could not support themselves with. This is where Alexander found himself. He became a butler, no great job, but one that did not require many skills. His primary duty was simply to follow instructions. Unskilled labor was something many immigrants found themselves doing even if they had previous experience in something in their home country. Like many other immigrants, Alexander also finds himself split from his family and anything he once found comfort in. But all this must be sacrificed if he wants to find a way for himself in this new country. His situation is not

that different from what many immigrants face in American society today.

The critique of gender roles in *This Way Out* is also still rel-
evant today. While women now have the right to vote and have
made much progress in the past century, they still often find
themselves not respected or taken as seriously as men. They are
still not in complete control of their own bodies, and are often
forced to listen to men who decide what happens to them. Much
like Lady Langlenshire, women today still want to be treated
with equality and acknowledged as the people they are. *This Way
Out* identifies social problems and calls for change, and over a
century later that need for change is still with us.

Bibliography

Smith, Geoffrey D. *American Fiction 1901-1925: A Bibliography.*

"Frederic S. Isham." Internet Broadway Database. The Broadway League, 2001. Web. 2 Apr. 2017.

"Timeline of the Legal History of Women in the United States." National Women's History Project. N.p., n.d. Web. 7 Apr. 2017.

"Early American Immigration Policies." U.S. Citizenship and Immigration Services. Department of Homeland Security, 4 Sept. 2015. Web. 7 Apr. 2017.

Timeline

1865   Frederic Isham is born in Detroit, Michigan

1875   Henrik Ibsen's *A Doll House* is published

1879   Minor v Happersett; The Supreme Court declares that despite the privileges and immunities clause, a state can prohibit a woman from voting

1895   Isham marries Helen Frue

1898   Henry James' *Turn of the Screw* is published

1900   Every state has passed legislature under New York's Married Women's Property Act (1839)

1904   The Panama Canal is started

1903   Isham's first novel, *Under the Rose*

1911   Edith Wharton's *Ethan Frome* is published

1917   The United States enters World War I

1917   *This Way Out* is first published

1920   The Nineteenth Amendment to the United States Constitution is ratified, giving women the right to vote

1922   Frederic Isham dies

1922   *3 Live Ghosts* is made into an Alfred Hitchcock film

1923   *Jack and Jill* is produced on Broadway

Chapter I
The Lady and the Porter

Lady Langlenshire looked up. "You wish to see me?" said the man. "Yes," said her ladyship. "Your ladyship has another errand for me?" "Perhaps—a long one." There was a peculiar accent in the patrician tones. "We shall see." "A long one?" repeated the fellow, studying her. "I said, "We shall see" observed the lady with a slight frown. The man shifted awkwardly and twirled his porter's cap in his hand. "You are not to do that,"said her ladyship. "What, my lady?" "Your hands—please keep them still." The man became immovable.

"That is better," said the lady. Then she was silent for a few moments, while her eyes passed disapprovingly over the details of the shabby furnishings of the somewhat abbreviated apartment, in that third-class hotel to which an untoward combination of circumstances had consigned her. Perhaps, at that moment, visions of ancestral halls and primrose meadows haunted her memory. The porter waited patiently. He was a burly fellow, with bent shoulders, and a countenance that might not have appeared so sodden except for a habit of keeping his mouth open. This gave him a stupid peasant look. He looked especially stupid, dull and of the proletariat, at the present moment, suffering possibly a slight embarrassment in that radiant, sylph-like presence. The lady's wandering attention again became focused upon him. She noted the bent shoulders, the open mouth, the grimy hands. Her gaze was singularly curious. "Your name is?"

"Alexander," he said. "You told me you are a Greek, I believe?" The heavy eyelids flickered beneath the clear and searching blue eyes of the lady. "Yes, your ladyship,"he said. A flash of merriment shone from the blue eyes. "Alexander the Great was a Greek, too, I believe," she ruminated aloud. "No relation, I suppose?" "Who was he?" said the man. "It is quite obvious you

1

are not related," said the lady, almost merrily. "Haven't you any illustrious ancestors, Alexander?" "No. Why?" The man stared stupidly. "Never mind," she observed. "Let the old ancestors go! If you only knew what a lot I've got, Alexander." "Yes," he assented, considering, no doubt, her ladyship was talking a great deal of nonsense. "Never mind," said the lady, reading the thought. "Don't try to think too hard, Alexander. It is racking to the brain."

"Yes; it's a bother to think," he said. "It is easier just to carry," she said, looking at the bent shoulders. "Has your ladyship a load for me?" "A load?"Again she laughed merrily. But her face soon became more sober. Her ladyship sometimes laughed when she did not feel like laughing. One laughs sometimes when the heart is very full. "A load?" she repeated. "Perhaps! Who shall say?" "Where shall I take it?" he demanded, more aggressively. "You are going too fast, Alexander," she said disapprovingly. "You must not try to hurry me. I am not accustomed to being hurried. You will please bear this in mind." "I have my work to do," he dared return. "And this is a part of your work. It is what you are paid for, and what I shall pay you for." The lady's tones were imperious. She had a very beautiful voice—young and silvery. It might have made a poet think of silvery bells on a frosty night. But Alexander was not a poet. "It is true your ladyship has tipped me well," he assented. "Yes; I usually do. By the way, how old are you?" "Twenty-four," said the fellow. "No more?" thought the lady, regarding the stooping figure. Twenty-four, and bent like that! "You must have worked hard all your life?" "Of course,"he answered simply. "What else is there to do?" "Nothing, I dare say." But the lady was thinking: "Straighten him, and he would make quite a figure of a man." He was very powerful, obviously. But with that open mouth and stupid expression he would always remain an uncouth son of the soil. It would take generations, no doubt, for the civilizing inner reconstruction. "I suppose you have the usual poor man's family, Alexander?"

"I have no family," he said. "Not even married?" "No." "Going to be, some day?" Languidly. "You need not be surprised at my questions. I always take an interest in the welfare of those who serve me. At home I consider myself, in a measure, morally responsible for the welfare of my servants. I am merely exercising my prerogative"— here she sighed—"away from home." "No; I'm not going to be married,"said the man, blinking stupidly. "There—there was a kitchen-girl—but—but she preferred the dishwasher. Women are all alike." "And so your heart is broken, and you have become a cynic?" Alexander did not answer. "At any rate you are free—perfectly free,"said my lady. "Yes; I don't have to bother about beating a wife when I come home." "Beating!"observed the lady, and surveyed the shambling, powerful figure. "If you beat any one I'm afraid it would hurt." "It would," said the fellow, grinning. "I think that afterward she behave herself." "No doubt!" My lady yawned. "That will do, Alexander. Here is a mark. Run away, now!" "Hasn't your ladyship something to carry?" In surprise. "Not just at present." "But—" He gazed at the coin. "I have done nothing." "Oh, yes, you have. Only you don't know it! Nor is it necessary to enlighten you. There are other ways of earning money than with your shoulders, Alexander. You have really served me. Possibly you have helped me amazingly. It is a little early definitely to determine."Alexander gazed at the lady steadfastly. "No, I'm not. In fact, I'm poignantly rational, at the moment, Alexander," said the lady. "Do you know what 'rational' means?"

Alexander shook his head. The lady regarded him. "How charming! You see, I have been used to clever men, and they bore one beyond endurance. To meet you is a refreshing change." The porter bowed stupidly. He did not know what else to do. "And now, go, most charming of porters," said the lady. "And let me dream that I am transported back to Arabian fantasies."Alexander bit the coin. "Yes, it's good," said the lady. And Alexander departed. The lady arose, and, going to the window, gazed out drearily. Then she went out. Her destination was the usual place—the police station. She waited her turn. It came at length. "Well?"said a harsh voice. "I am here to report." Quietly. "Lift up your veil." She did. "'Estelle Langlenshire,' " he said, reading the police paper she handed him. "Twenty-one, Single." "How do you live?" Bruskly. "I had a little money with me. I am conserving it very carefully." "Humph!"For the moment he studied her. "You may go—for now!" "You mean there may be a change later?"Drawing her breath quickly. "How can I say?" Impatiently. "It is possible?" "All things are possible." "Probable, then? I may be deprived of my— my liberty?" He made a movement. "Others are waiting. You are detaining — Guten Tag!" "Good day," she said and left.

CHAPTER II
A STARTLING PROPOSAL

The hotel she once more sent for Alexander. She had seemingly regained her lightness of spirits. Not a worry seemed to cloud her fair brow; no light of trouble or tragedy lingered in the violet eyes. She had lighted a cigarette and disposed her lithe form daintily on a couch.

"Alexander," she said, "you are going to be married." "So?" said Alexander. His tones were heavy and sodden. What was the joke? The lady smiled. "You do not ask whom you are going to marry?" "Does that matter?" said Alexander, thinking her doubtlessly bereft of her senses. "You mean that since you were disappointed in love—since the scrub-lady 'threw you down,' as our American friends say, all women look alike to you?" she observed vivaciously.

"Suppose so," mumbled Alexander guardedly. The lady shifted; a dainty bit of hosiery was momentarily visible, but that evanescent gleam was lost upon Alexander. "I am pleased to find your mental attitude what it is," said the lady. As Alexander probably did not know what was his mental attitude, he did not answer. "The lady you are to marry will be revealed to you at the proper moment. Meanwhile you are to make arrangements." "Arrangements?" "With the Greek priest, of course!" "Priest?" The lady's tone began to sound as if she meant it. "There is a Greek priest, isn't there?" "Oh, yes." A bit dazed. "And a Greek church?" "Oh, yes." "You go there sometimes?" Severely. "Sometimes." Dully. "And know the good priest?"

"Yes." "Good!" She spoke gaily. "Now, listen: You are to go to him. You are to tell him you have fallen deeply in love." "Eh?" Alexander's eyes began to gleam resentfully. "You can tell him, can't you?" "A big lie, like that?" Alexander laughed hoarsely. "Stupid!" The lady lifted a tolerant eyebrow. "What's a little lie like that?

5

The principal thing is, you aren't really in love. You don't have to be. Get that firmly in mind. Now, don't you feel easier?" "I suppose so." Dubiously. "There's no 'suppose' about it. You do." Aggressively. "Get that thought firmly, and don't make the mistake of trying to think for yourself. It would be an awful error and get you nowhere. Let others think for you, and perhaps you will amount to something some day, Alexander. A great many people become great by eliminating their own mental processes. Use other people's brains; that's the Jacob's ladder to the heaven of large attainments. It's not what you do. It's what others do for you."

Alexander stared, as well he might. Did one- tenth of this filter into his dull brain? The lady laughed deliciously. "Hand me my cigarette case, Alexander." Alexander tried to, and dropped it. "How adorably useful!" purred the lady. Alexander managed finally to deliver the case. "Where were we?" said the lady of the couch. "Oh, yes! You had gone to the priest. You had told him you were head-over-heels in love—"Alexander made a movement. "Don't interrupt!"Imperiously. "You tell the good priest you are in love, because she is so beautiful—" "Oh!" From Alexander. A snort! "Silence!" From the lady. "Anyhow, what is the difference whether she is, or not. You like money, Alexander?" Insidiously. "Oh!" said Alexander, brightening a bit.

"You do. It's your god. It's every man's. It comes first and last. Love?" She made a movement. "But you've got to pretend, Alexander." "Pretend?" "That you have won her—your scrub-lady!" Alexander made a sound. "You are to seem radiant with happiness—that is your attitude before the priest. Of course you couldn't really be radiant, but maybe you could take some of that bend out of your shoulders. Do you think you could stand up like a man in love?" Again Alexander made a sound. "Never mind," said the lady. "I suppose it's there to stay. Only you are to tell the priest you want to be married at once. You can't wait. It will be impossible. What you want, you want. You are distracted to possess it immediately." "What I want?" said Alexander. "Well, what I am telling you you want! Did you ever dream of having a thousand marks?" "I once saved a hundred. But a thousand—" "Two thousand—that's what I meant to say."

"Two!"Alexander breathed hard. The lady obviously grew more interesting in his eyes. "What could you do with two thousand?" "Do?" He stared at that figure alluring—a golden princess now. "I wouldn't have to do any thing—to carry—to blacken boots—to be cuffed by the head porter! I could have all I wanted to eat—" "And drink," added the fair temptress. "Drink?" Alexander moistened his lips. Dreams of deep potations no doubt assailed him. The lady's red lips curved scornfully; then tolerantly. What right had she to sit in judgment? Hadn't most of her aristocratic ancestors been four- or five-bottle men? "Why should I chide you, Alexander," she observed softly, "for the manner in which you anticipate spending the reward I am going to bestow upon you, for bestowing upon me your name, your fortunes, and, last but not least, your non-affections?" "Oh, it's you," said Alexander. So she was the one who wanted to marry him? "But why?"

"Pooh!" she returned. "Why get categorical? What must be, must be! Isn't that sufficient? Think of the reward, if you must think at all."Alexander did. He asked no more questions. "That is well," said the lady. "I sure get the two thousand?" "On the word of the daughter of a belted earl!" said the lady. That sounded good enough for Alexander. "When you want it to take place?" he said stoically. "Say day after to-morrow. Or the day after that! You see, I have my trousseau to prepare." "Which?" said Alexander. "A wedding-gown, in keeping with my new lofty station,"-said the lady. "Oh, you mean scrub-woman's clothes?" said Alexander practically. "Maybe I swipe some for you, somewhere." "No; please don't swipe my wedding-garments, Alexander," said the lady. "Have you no sentiment? Please acquire them by purchase from some old-clothes man." Slipping him a few pieces of money. "Only be very secretive. There is need." "You bet! I get you," said Alexander. Lust for the reward was already in his eyes. "I handle this thing mighty well. You leave to me." The lady sighed. Anyhow, he looked very big and powerful, as he spoke. It would be nice to shift some of the responsibility if she could. If? With Alexander's brawn and her brains something might be accomplished. "And now trot along and see the priest," she said.

Alexander trotted. The die was cast. She had burned her bridges.

Chapter III
The Flight

A train speeding northward! A third- class compartment! Hour after hour the train had been speeding. Now suddenly it stopped. "The frontier!" A guard looked in; the door opened; the people got out—a slow business! One man—a big fellow— yet slept in a corner, and snored—or seemed to. "Here, wake your good man, woman!" cried the guard to her at the slumber- er's side. She did. The uncouth-looking fellow rubbed his eyes sleepily. Then he reached up for a bundle of old duds. Then the man, followed by the woman, approached Officialdom. The ex- amination of their papers took some moments. Once the wom- an seemed to sway from weariness, or some other emotion. Her hand clutched the man's arm; he coolly thrust the bundle of old duds into her arms.

"Here, you hold 'em," he said. The "duds" made quite an armful; held to her breast, they partly concealed the woman's face. "Learn 'em young," said the man, with a sodden grin at Of- ficialdom. The peasants' philosophy! Start woman carrying things as soon as she's married and she's more likely to keep up the habit. Officialdom laughed harshly. It understood that ungentle peasant philosophy. Hadn't it been grinding down womankind for generations—keeping woman "in her place"? Trust your son of the soil for that! "Just married, eh?" said Officialdom, survey- ing a number of papers. "Yes." With a loutish grin. Officialdom peered around the "old duds." "Shy little dove!" "You bet. I tell her what she get, she look at a man." Coarsely. "Beginning right, all right!"Again the woman's figure seemed to sway.

Alexander's big fingers gripped her arm. At the moment they seemed to grip her cruelly. He felt her straighten magically. Again that hateful laugh. "She mind me—you bet!" said Alexander. "Well, get on," said Officialdom. No doubt Officialdom deemed this a perfect and ideal way to start the honeymoon. There seemed to exist such a perfect understanding. Oh, happy bride! Bride of the soil! "Don't you hear the gentleman say 'Get on'?" said Alexander. And to emphasize their newfound relations and his authority, he gave her a shove. Now, no one had ever shoved Lady Langlenshire before. It was a novel experience. By indulging in this little connubial commonplace liberty, Alexander almost overstepped his mark. Almost the lady hurled the old duds at his feet. She had felt strangely weak and "droopy" at the moment Alexander had first placed the bundle in her arms, and his unexpected and ignominious action had oddly revived her. So, too, that subsequent conversation with Officialdom.

Indignation had superseded any fears and misgivings that had momentarily assailed her. Alexander's perfectly natural conduct under these circumstances had acted as so many dashes of cold water upon her. Alexander had really served her, and saved her perhaps from betraying herself; but when he gave her that shove he went almost too far. She did, however, manage to control herself, and somehow to move mechanically away from the gate and Officialdom. Her feelings need not be described. She was still carrying the old duds—she, the daughter of a proud earl! Alexander came sauntering behind. Now they were on the street. Alexander still sauntered at his ease. Then he stopped to strike a match and light his pipe. She could picture him smoking. That was good; excellent. Several blocks she moved on. If only some of her friends could have seen her in that peasant garb, with Alexander's old duds held to her aristocratic breast.

Suddenly she stopped. Alexander came up. He was smoking contentedly. A moment the lady regarded him; then suddenly she cast the vile bundle at his feet. "Take it!" she almost hissed. Alexander looked surprised. "Eh?" he said. "Take it!" she repeated dramatically. "Eh?" he said once more, his mouth drooping still farther. "And walk behind!" "But in my country——" he began helplessly. "Where a porter should!" interrupted the lady. Revenge for all she had endured was in her tones. She had gone back a few hundred years that day, to what women had been wont to endure. In Alexander she had beheld the prehistoric monster of her sex. She would set the big, bungling animal where he belonged. "Pick it up," she repeated imperiously. And Alexander was so surprised he obeyed. At the hotel, the lady announced her name and condition, and, briefly, vouchsafed a few whys and wherefores to explain her humble attire. The landlord was sympathetic, as landlords are apt to be with nobility in distress, especially when it can pay its bills. "And now," said the lady, "have you a nice room?" "A cheap one will do," said Alexander, at that moment insinuating himself upon the scene with the old duds. "Who is this person?" said the landlord, frowning. "It's—it's the man," said the lady. "A porter?" "The porter," she breathed. "Husband," mumbled Alexander. "Of convenience," laughed the lady. "You know our understanding? The reward you are to get?" "Three thousand," said Alexander, who had obviously been thinking a good deal, while en route to the hotel with the bundle. "If you have that, you have more."

"Why for I give up much, for a little? I have you. Why not keep?" "Horrors!" said the lady. "Scoundrel!" said the landlord, sensing the situation. Alexander grinned unctuously. "Maybe, we go to Greece some day. You learn to work. Best for all women to work!" "In the fields?" said the lady, elevating her patrician brow. "Sure," said Alexander. "Is this a dream?" said the lady. "This new attitude of yours! You, whom I thought sans guile!" "I know which side my bread is greased," observed Alexander. "Horrors!"

said the lady again. "At least say 'buttered.'" "Same thing," remarked Alexander placidly. "Let me tell you, Alexander," said the lady reprovingly, "you are playing a very dangerous game. And one which will only react upon your-self. Have you any porters?" Turning to the landlord. "Yes, your ladyship." "Oh, I don't want to marry them!" Quickly. "One porter is quite enough. I do not wish to emulate the Merry Princess and the Six Grimey Porters of Bagdad. Are your porters strong?" "Powerful," said the landlord. "Call them in," said the lady. He did. One was almost as big as Alexander. "Throw him out," said the landlord, indicating Alexander. For thus he interpreted the lady's intention. "One moment," she said. "Ask them to withdraw, for the present." The landlord obeyed. "Now, Alexander," said the lady, "will you peaceably depart, for. the time being, or be forcibly ejected?" "You mean they throw me out?" "Yes." "Maybe I throw them all out," said Alexander, with superb assurance.

"All of them?" said the lady. "The whole blame bunch," said Alexander. "I bust up the whole crowd." "Could you?" said the lady blithely. "I wonder? But that would be positively Homeric. Bust up the whole crowd! You, alone!" "I clean out whole wineshop, once. Eight men! Break everything," said Alexander. "This is interesting," said her ladyship. "According to all the rules of romance you should do something interesting—something big and bizarre!" "I'll settle him," said the landlord in an exasperated tone, and seized Alexander. Alexander gave a hoarse, harsh laugh of unnatural glee. "Ho, ho!" he guffawed, and then he seized the landlord by the seat of his trousers and the next moment was performing dumb-bell exercises with him. The lady burst into laughter; Alexander, at that moment, was magnificent. She forgot about his cupidity, his treachery, his guile I Alexander at length set down the host, who looked sick and seemed dizzy. He could hardly stand. "I go now," said Alexander. "Where's the nearest wineshop?" "A—round the—corner," the other managed to sputter. "I don't know when I come back," said Alexander. "I my

own master. Do what I please!" "Of course,"said the lady faintly.
"You don't want me to come back?" he asked. "On the contrary, I
should miss you dreadfully! I don't know when I have been more
entertained." "Oh, you see me again, all right," said Alexander
naïvely. "I keep my eye, on good thing!" And strode out. "Isn't he
delightful?" said the lady. But what the landlord said is neither
here nor there. Alexander showed his independence once more,
by staying out all night. The lady could not get a boat that first
day, so had to wait until the next.

Whatever his adventures, and whether Alexander slept on a
bench or on the beach, he appeared in the morning, spick and
span—for him —and apparently as fresh as a daisy. In fact, dis-
sipation and riotous living seemed to agree with Alexander; he
looked like a man who had retired seasonably, slept soundly, and
had arisen with a good conscience in the morning. No one, to
gaze upon him, would ever have suspected him of wild debauch-
es and unstinted revelry. The lady had left word that he was to be
admitted to the hotel parlor, and so great was her social prestige
and high standing in the aristocratic world that her wishes were
respected, if secretly resented, by the disgruntled keeper of the
establishment. He gave Alexander a wide berth, as that individual entered with the tread of a gladiator. Then the proprietor
shrugged his shoulders.. Her ladyship was incomprehensible; but
she had seemed that to many people, before this.

Alexander found a transformed lady. She had evidently been
shopping, and had established a line of substantial credit somewhere. She wore a wonderful Paris gown, and the daintiest of
shoes. Her golden hair was no longer brushed straight back but
was an aureole of light. Alexander looked at the gown, and then
he looked at the shoes. "Where you get all that?" he said. "At
the shops." "Cost a lot!" "Quite a lot." Alexander pondered.
"Good wives, in my country, don't spend money," he observed.
"I suppose not," said the lady calmly. "No woman could work, in
that,"was Alexander's next comment. "No?" Alexander pointed

an accusing finger. "Too small,"he said with a frown. "My shoes? Pardon me," gaily, "a perfect fit!"

"What you do with the others?" "I threw them away." "Good shoes, like that!" Indignantly. "You will find them reposing in some rubbish heap." Tranquilly. "Rubbish heap!" cried Alexander. "Where?" "I really couldn't locate it for you." Languidly. Alexander pondered some more. Apparently he gave up the shoes for lost. "You throw away the dress, too?" "Of course." "Fine clothes!" Alexander looked depressed. "I not like wife, like that," he said. "So sorry you disapprove of me, Alexander!" The lady was beginning to enjoy herself once more. The psychology of Alexander was mildly entertaining. "You keep shawl?"said Alexander. "Maybe, I get something for that." "No, Alexander." He breathed deeply. "All those fine things!"

The lady laughed. Not once had Alexander really looked at her! And yet the long mirror reflected a radiant presence; a vision of youth and loveliness! In one way, there was something reassuring about Alexander. "When we leave?" he next asked. "Are you so anxious to go? Are the wineshops not to your liking?" she asked frivolously. "Wineshops all right." "But you are thinking of the reward? The sooner we go, the quicker you get that?" "No use waiting for money," said Alexander. "Didn't I earn it?" "You did." "If I thought you were trying to get out of paying—" he began. "Oh, Alexander!" interrupted the lady reproachfully. "Women like to cheat!" "Not all, surely?" argued the lady, in that same sad tone. "You surely would, except some of us?"

"Blame the few" said Alexander. "About all alike!" "Say not so," she breathed. "Do not put us all in the same category." "Anyhow, I stick by. Where you go, I go!" He grinned uncouthly. "No cheat, if you don't get the chance. I stick by, until I get cold cash! Maybe longer!" "How mercenary! And with the stage all set for—romance! The novelists would never for give you, Alexander." "Romance?" said Alexander, puckering his brow. "What's that?" "What, indeed?" said the lady. "A delight that dwells in the

shadow of a rose; a thrill that mounts on a moonbeam!" "Crazi-
ness," remarked Alexander, looking at the lady. Then he rattled
several coins in his pocket. "When I got them, I got something."
"Is it Alexander I hear speaking, or the World?" murmured the
lady sadly. "Bah! Everybody know that," said Alexander. "It is
the World!" The lady sighed; then arose, with a light laugh. "And
now let us go aboard." "The steamer?" "Yes, I have two tickets."
"Then give me mine." Alexander held out his hand. "Oh, no,"
said the lady, "you have to see after my luggage first. You see, I
told the hotel man, I have my own private porter." "Me?" "You!"
As she spoke she smiled sweetly. First victory of the day, for her!
And she had purchased a particularly heavy trunk—one made of
tin. "Whew! that darn heavy trunk!" said Alexander, breathing
hard at the wharf. "I thought you were so strong," said the lady.

"I thought you could clear out a whole wineroom of loafers,
all by yourself." "You pick out heaviest trunk on purpose!" Suspiciously. "How can you attribute such motives to me?" she said
chidingly. "Drop him, from top of building, no hurt," said Alexander. "That's just the point," said the lady. "But here I ascend!" A
deck-hand took the trunk from Alexander and the latter followed
the lady up a gangplank. The lady, with her ticket, passed inspec-
tion and got by, but Alexander was not permitted to pass. "This
calls for steerage," said the man. "Steerage?" said Alexander. "Yes;
up forward with you, my man!" "But—I want to be near her,"
expostulated Alexander. "You can't—on this!" "But, she buy me
this. A fine trick!"

"I can't waste any more time on you. Down you go!" And
Alexander did. On the tiny steerage deck, forward, he looked up
and saw the lady and gritted his teeth. A mean trick, he repeated; and he, her husband! Again Alexander looked up; some one
dropped a cigar ash and some of it got in Alexander's eye. He
shook his fist at the individual. Did he hear a light musical laugh?
He would almost have sworn to the fact. "I fix you," muttered
Alexander, looking up at the alluring image of the lady leaning

against the rail, so far above him. But she did not look down; she seemed otherwise engrossed as the ship got under way. Alexander settled himself upon a hard bench and gave himself up to apparently moody reflections. The lady moved away. Now Alexander seemed a statue of patience and resignation. He didn't see the lady again for quite a long time, and then under circumstances most unusual.

Chapter IV
Aquatic

The ship had struck a mine.

This, in itself, was not so unusual; rather to be expected, in this mad, mad world! My lady had been in her stateroom when it happened; her door had been jammed by the force of the concussion and it was some time before she could get out. When she did reach the deck, the life-boats had left; she called, but no one heard. The ship lurched and she sprang wildly into the sea. Then her brain became blurred, and after that there was a blank. When she opened her eyes and consciousness began to return to her, she saw Alexander. She did not feel exactly surprised; she had become rather accustomed to seeing him; he had grown into a species of habit with her. "So here you are again?" she observed. "Yes," said Alexander, not quite so harshly as usual.

"Looks like fate, doesn't it?" said the lady. Alexander did not answer. He was not given to philosophizing. "I suppose I should say 'Where am I?'" murmured the lady. "Humph!" said Alexander, but still not so harshly as his wont. "Though," she went on, "the query would be entirely superfluous. It is quite apparent, isn't it?" "It is." conceded Alexander. "We—we are on a hatch, or something." "Life-raft," corrected Alexander. "How—how odd! Perhaps I should say, how convenient—I mean, the life-raft," observed the lady, rather incoherently. Then she saw she was fastened to the raft by a rope, passed around her slender waist. Alexander was unfastened, sitting at his ease; he seemed able to stay on, without any extraneous aid. For a landsman, he appeared quite at home. The lady looked at the rope.

"I don't remember doing that," she said. "What?" asked Alexander. "Tying it." "Don't you?" He grinned. "Oh, women do a lot of things they—" "Stop!" Imperiously. "If there's one thing I dislike more than any other, it's deception—or attempted de-

17

ception," she added. "You tied it." "Of course!" Nonchalantly. "Then why didn't you say so at once?" Accusingly. "Much talk about nothing," said Alexander. "You think it was nothing to have tied me to the raft so I couldn't slide into the sea?" Alexander shrugged. My lady's eyes began to shine. She began to see vaguely—very vaguely—new qualities in Alexander. Alexander put out his big hands. "It was easier than to have to hold you on," he said simply. My lady subsided. So? He looked upon her as a bale of hay, or something of the kind. That was the kind of hero your clod of a peasant was! My lady, be it understood, had been accustomed to admiration, adulation, adoration. All kinds of men had desired her, for all manner of reasons. She had been given to understand, in the heydey of her triumphs, not so long ago, that she had what might be called a species of "universal appeal."

The poet found in her pure and lofty inspiration; to the musician she suggested blithe rondeau or mad variations; the writer made her the· heroine of his' plots; the statesman had discovered in her a born aptitude for intrigue and diplomatic chess-games; the libertine and man of the world—but why go on? She gazed at Alexander with cold displeasure. "A bale of hay!" Alexander didn't blink. "I no want you to slide off,"he muttered. "How kind!" "Oh, it wasn't any bother!" "I'm so glad of that!" "Pooh!" said Alexander. "You're again saying things you don't mean."

"And why shouldn't I?" she challenged him. "If it wasn't for the illusions—" "Pooh!" said Alexander once more, balancing himself with difficulty as the raft gave a swoop sidewise. "Look out!" she said, expecting to see him pitch into the sea. "You say 'Look out!' when I don't need"—regaining his balance—"longer to 'look out'!" "Forgive me, for trying to warn you." "That's all right!" "Next time you can go overboard!" Sharply. "Oh, no, I stay here! That you do not give me—the slip!" The lady made a gesture. Then she thought deeply. "Did you save my life?" "I hauled you from the water." "How did you happen to see me?" "I climb up on deck, to wait and watch for you. Every one get off, in life-boats. Every one is saved."

"I wonder why you do not come? The boats go away. I wait." "You feared to lose me?" "Of course, we must not part." "I think I understand! Go on! You could not bear that we should part!— and then?" "The fog come down. I call out to the lifeboats, but no answer! Every one is saved but you and me! You have not left. I was sure." "You said that before." "I look for you; I do not find you; I search for you. The ship go down, and then—then"— the fog seemed to have got into Alexander's throat—"I bump into you, in the water." "Yes?" The lady's voice involuntarily grew a little softer. "I am very glad!" "Were you?" said the lady with sudden curiosity. "You bet; I couldn't let you go!" With a grin in which cupidity and cunning mingled.

"You are alluding to mercenary reasons?" "Does that mean money?" "It does. So it wasn't me you were saving. It was the reward?" Alexander did not answer directly. "I look after you," he said vaguely. "Cheer up!" "I am cheerful," the lady protested. "When I think of all it means to you, I feel quite safe in your presence, my dear Alexander!" "Now you talk sense!" "Indeed, I believe that with you at my side I am safer than I would be on the streets of London town. You won't let anything happen to me, will you, Alexander—my hero?" "Bet your life I won't!" The lady shuddered. "Isn't that—land, Alexander?" Alexander looked. Then he moved over to the lady and lifted her, from where she was half- lying. Her eyes widened, but otherwise she was perfect-ly passive. The wet dress clung to her form, her hair was down, and she had a feeling distinctively mermaidish!

She felt as if she ought to be able to slip into the water and swim around down there among the shells and other things. "May I ask your intentions?" she said, to Alexander, looking down at the muscular arm with which he half-sustained her. "Wait!" said Al-exander. The lady held her breath. Her hair flew into Alexander's face. He brushed it away. "This is rather sudden!" breathed the lady. "What?" said Alexander. "This—your arm!" "Keep still!" "I am. There—there isn't any room to move away!" The arm tightened. The lady straightened. "How—"she began, with fire in her eye. Then his purpose dawned upon her. He was only trying to untie the knots of the line about her waist.

The strain had drawn them tight and the task was not easy for his big fingers, chilled by the sea. "Are you going to throw me back?" One could never tell what Alexander would do next. "Don't talk nonsense! I tied them too tight!" he grumbled. "You were so anxious I wouldn't fall off? If you don't want to throw me overboard, may I ask why you are untying the rope?" "You'll see!" "Perhaps I can help?" "You?" Scornfully. "Oh, little fingers can, sometimes, do what big fingers can't!" She did try to help. Little fingers mingled with big fingers. Then, somehow, the knots came undone. "You see?" Triumphantly. "Bah! You think you do that?" said Alexander. "Do you deny me any of the credit?"

Alexander did not answer. He tied the line around his waist. "Oh!" said the lady. "How heroic! But perhaps you think: 'Turn about is fair play?' And so it is! I will try and stick on!" Still Alexander did not answer—with words! He plunged into the sea. Then he began to swim toward the land, slowly drawing the raft after him. The lady clapped her hands. Alexander, at that moment, was superb, cleaving the waves with the vigor of a Neptune.

CHAPTER V
THE NYMPH AND THE WATER-GOD

They reached the shore at last. "What a charming method of transportation!" said the lady. "I am sure you must have been a water-god in some other reincarnation, Alexander!" Alexander did not answer. He lay prone on the strand, his face to the sky, his great chest laboring; his breath coming in gasps. "Oh!" said the lady, forgetting ironical amusement. What should she do? What did they do, in the story-books—the heroines? When Alexander recovered, he should find his head in her lap. She didn't wish to proceed to that extreme but she felt it incumbent to be polite. His exertions in her behalf had been herculean. My how the man must like money! She moved forward, politely, with vague intentions, but Alexander waved her away.

Her eyes flashed. Had he misinterpreted her. action? Had he dared think she had intended to act like the conventional heroine—about his head? She gazed at him now, sans pity! Let him perish, the monster! Alexander began to recover, while the lady sat on a rock. At last he arose and shook himself. "Some pull, that!" he said. "Yes; you'll have earned the reward!" Alexander frowned. "Extra work!" he said. "You mean you did not figure on anything like this when you accepted the contract to marry me? You infer that you have been working overtime?" Alexander nodded approvingly. His shirt was torn open, and a bit of his magnificent torso was visible. But though Alexander might look like an antique Greek water-god, he acted like a modern Greek land-shark. It was hard to play nymph to such a water-god. Though he had lost most of his "stoop," or crick in his back, superinduced by carrying trunks up and down stairs! In fact, the sea seemed to have magically washed some of the "bend" away, and straightened his spine.

On the rock, the lady ruminated. She dropped the subject of

extra reward. Alexander, however, was not disposed so lightly to abandon the topic. "How much extra, you think?" Oh, what a bargaining look shone from the "water-god's eyes now! "Suppose we leave the precise details to be determined later?" Alexander was about to expostulate, but she cut him short. "Don't you see, I could promise anything?" she said. "After all, it's purely a matter of good faith." "Suppose so!" His voice implied he recognized the weakness of his position. Trust a woman! Yet, what else was there to do? Alexander's face grew sad—almost pathetic! "Yes, I know it's hard," breathed the lady. "But pull yourself together! That drooping manner ill becomes one designed by nature for the exploits of a Ulysses!"

"Who's him?" said Alexander listlessly. "A countryman of yours!" "Never met him!" "I suppose not. He was a great man!" "You mean, a big man?" "Very big!" "Big as me?" "Quite!" "I think I could whip him." Boastfully. "I look him up when we go back to my country." "We?" Elevating an eyebrow. "Sure! You don't like to go?" Challengingly. "Nothing would give me greater pleasure!" Hastily, for Alexander's tone was very truculent. "But meanwhile, don't you think we had better consider the immediate, not the far-distant and uncertain future? I don't wish to appear trite, but where are we?" "Don't know!"

"Well, let's walk along," said the lady. The beach was quite rocky. Above, a sheer cliff loomed. The walking was bad, especially for high heels, and the lady had not gone far when she slipped and would have fallen, except for Alexander. "Those no-account shoes!" he grumbled. "You no slip with good shoes, you throw away!" "I believe I have turned my ankle," answered the lady, and slid to a shelf of stone. "Eh?" Alexander actually. showed sudden sympathy. He forgot to reprove her further about the "good shoes" she had thrown away, in ash-heap or garbage-can. "Oh, it's not a real sprain," she reassured him with a silvery laugh, somewhat forced. "Don't worry! You won't have to carry me! I'll rest a bit, though, and then it will be quite all right, I am sure." "I look and see!" "No, no! I know you should, of course, be kneeling at my feet, and all that, but it is quite unnecessary." "Nonsense talk!" Gruffly. "Let me see!" "I decline! There's no movie-picture man near." "I see, anyway!" said Alexander. And did! It was useless to resist. He untied her shoe—not ungently—and removed it. "Take off your stocking!" he next commanded, and she obeyed.

Perhaps she was rather apprehensive just what would happen if she didn't. "Hum!" he said, and felt the ankle. The lady winced, but whether at the twinge of pain or from the touch of those coarse fingers, who shall say? "Not bad!" diagnosed Doctor Alexander, and took out a big red handkerchief from his blouse. The "bandanna" was as big as four ordinary men's handkerchiefs. The lady shuddered. Its colors fairly shrieked. "Take it away!" Faintly. "For why? You do what I say!"

"I—I suppose I must." "Of course!" He bound up the ankle—rather skillfully. His fingers weren't half so rough as she had expected. Also, she noted with a certain relief, the bandanna had just been laundered. "There! That good job!" boasted Alexander. "Me once doctor! Horse-doctor; sheep-doctor!" The lady was past shivering. Horse-doctor; sheep-doctor! In which category did she come? She felt like a lost lamb; a high-bred lamb, of course! "This job extra, of course!" said Alexander. The lady almost shrieked. "Oh, Alexander, you will be the death of me!" "For why?" queried Alexander. "Why you laugh?" "Why, indeed? I know it is no laughing matter." "Unless you think it funny, because you"— he paused—"intend to cheat me? You think how my face look when you say:'Kick him out! You have three, four, five servants?"

"Quite that number, my sweet Alexander!" "Perhaps, you say that, to them?" "You wrong me! Such lack of confidence in a—a wife, is totally uncalled for. You should have faith in me—believe!" Alexander tapped his chest. "Me look out for myself! You bet!" "Then all is well," said the lady. "Or as well as could be for two people marooned on a barren coast! Without food or drink! Which reminds me I am very hungry. As the big magician you couldn't by any chance rub a magical lamp, Alexander, and procure for me a broiled chicken?" "No chicken!" said Alexander. "Something better!" And took from his blouse a mighty sausage! A king of sausages; a Gargantuan sausage! "How perfectly delightful!" said the lady. "Me grab him, before leaving the ship!"-said Alexander proudly. "No steerage sausage!" Contemptuously. "Me grab him, in first-class place! No one to keep me out!"A moment he eyed her with rising resentment. "That nice trick of yours, shoving me in steerage!"

"Why speak of the past?" Quickly. "Are not our present perplexities sufficient? Perhaps we shall both die of exposure. Indeed it is quite likely!" "Nice trick!" muttered Alexander, not disposed to forget the past as readily as the lady was. "Maybe, I take him back?" Eying the sausage which he had placed at the lady's side. "Say not so! Would you starve me? If you did you could not collect the reward." This argument seemed to carry weight. Alexander hesitated. "Please forgive me," said the lady. "Is it not the privilege of the strong to forgive the weak? And you—you are so strong! Did I not feel it when you towed me ashore on the raft! How your mighty arms cleft the waves! How I rejoiced in the spectacle of the same! A Titan of the deep! Jove, come down!"-Alexander blinked. The lady's words would have staggered any mere man.

But having blinked, Alexander quickly recovered himself. If her blandishments had been almost lost upon him, that practical remark concerning the reward had not been without effect. "Eat away," he said. "Me good husband! No starve wife! Bully good husband, you bet!" "It's nice to be so well-satisfied with yourself, isn't it?" said the lady. "But what a perfectly charming sausage! I feared, at first—its ingredients. But now—" Her tones grew lively. "Genuine foi gras and bona-fide truffles!" "Yes; I swiped it, first-class place!" "A high-bred, patrician sausage!" ruminated the lady. Alexander took, from his trousers pocket, a small jar. "Marmalade!" he said. "How perfectly delightful! Why, you're a regular walking delicatessen-shop! Have you anything else concealed on your person?" "No time to get more!" "Well, I'll spread the marmalade on the sausage, I'm sure the combination will be ideal. Meanwhile, you might walk along and try to find out where we are. And by the time you return I'm sure the ankle will be quite serviceable." For once, Alexander seemed to find the lady's words sensible. At any rate, he did not controvert her; he even went further. He acted upon the suggestion. Abruptly turning, without another glance for her, Alexander walked away. The lady watched him disappear around a bend. Suddenly, she ceased eating. "Oh, how funny!" She looked around her. "That I did not notice before!" Then she began to laugh. "I suppose I was so confused and preoccupied!" She looked around again. "One would be!" She put down the sausage. "This is, positively, the best ever!" Her glance was fastened on a slight opening at the foot of the cliff, near by. "The Witch's Eye!" she observed.

"That is it—indubitably! And it was looking at me, all the time! Probably it was witch's magic that caused me to slip!" The lady got up, abandoning the remains of the patrician sausage and the marmalade on the shelf of rock. "I'd like to see Alexander's face, when he comes and finds me gone!" she murmured. "Oh, this is as good as hare-and-hounds. He has me; he has me not! Has—not!" The lady walked to the crevice, or "Eye." She limped slightly but was in the best of spirits. Beyond the "Eye," fringed with dark bushes, the opening widened just as she knew it would, and farther along there was a gully. A path led to the top. "Oh, Alexander, I can just see you!" gurgled the lady, as she started up the path, carrying one shoe. At the top of the gully which presently she reached, the path led across a broad meadow, and beyond, at the verge of a park, a noble dwelling arose. Langlenshire house! Built in the time of the first of the Georges! The lady, pausing at the gate, poised on one foot, gazed with pleased interest upon the stately and charming pile. "What an odd way to come home!" she thought.

Chapter VI
The 'Uman Tiger

"Is there anythink, ma'am?" A man stepped from the little lodge as the lady found herself thus strangely and unexpectedly entering her own estates, after a prolonged and somewhat enforced absence therefrom. "Nothing special, thank you, James!" "Good 'eavens! Is it really your ladyship?" "I believe so," said the lady, hobbling toward the house. "Do not let your surprise overcome you, James!" James strove to relapse into the impassive model servant. "Yes, I just landed," observed the lady. "Quite so, your ladyship! At Folkstone, perhaps?" "No, James!" But her ladyship offered no further information, and James trotted along by her side, fairly bursting with curiosity. The lady divined and smiled.

She rather enjoyed the situation. She wouldn't have missed coming home like that for a great deal. "Good morning, Pelton," she said to the butler, at the front door. "Or is it afternoon?" Pelton nearly fell over as the lady entered her ancestral hall. "Yes, the same old place!" she said. "We'll have to shift those suits of armor, Pelton. They do look so tired, always standing in the same place! Kindly see that it is done, Pelton!" "Yes, your ladyship!" Pelton managed to ejaculate, his eyes sticking out like those of an excited frog. "So glad to see your ladyship once more." "Yes, I understand!" Languidly. "Thank you, so much!" "Your ladyship's luggage?" Pelton was just able to stammer, gazing, not without horror, at the shoe her ladyship was carrying in her hand. "There is no luggage! So inconvenient to be bothered with luggage, Pelton, you know!" "Quite so, your ladyship!" stammered Pelton.

"The rooms are in order?" "Oh, yes, especially your ladyship's apartments which Jane has looked after, especially—" "Thank you so much, Jane!" As that person bustled up. "Yes, you're glad to see me and all that," she interrupted the hysterical Jane. "Consider it said! Thank you—so much!" "Is there anything, your ladyship?" began the bewildered Jane. "Can you ask?" Reproachfully. "Is there? Think!" Jane thought; Pelton thought; others, peering in, thought. "There is something. What would it be? Concentrate!" They did—painfully! "Oh!"said her ladyship, reproachfully once more. They wriggled like worms—more and more miserably. Then a great light burst upon Jane. "Tea!" she exclaimed triumphantly. "Of course!" Her ladyship beamed. "What else could it be? For a moment I began to feel like an alien in a foreign land."

"Serve it at once, Jane, in my apartments, while I snuggle into a few dry clothes." They all vanished except Pelton, whom her ladyship yet detained. "Pelton, I am expecting, shortly, a caller." "Yes, your ladyship." "A big rough-looking man! He will probably be very angry." "A gentleman, your ladyship?" "You would hardly call him that, Pelton. You would, probably, consider him a very common person. Your inclination would be to send him about his business." "And am I not to do so?" asked the bewildered Pelton. "For your owrt sake I would advise you not to." "For my sake?" "He will arrive, as I have told you, probably in an uncommon temper. As he is very strong, I tremble to think what might happen to you, were you to oppose him."

"You see, he is a person bound to have his own way!" "'Is way!" said Pelton. "He might be capable of proceeding to any extremity," said the lady. "The limit—do you understand?" "Your ladyship means—h'assassination?" "I think it is quite possible. You see, he possibly thinks he has a grievance. He may even imagine—indeed, I think it is quite likely—he has been cheated. He is a man who might—to use your expression, Pelton —h'assassinate, under the circumstances!" "H'I'd better call the magistrate! H'I'd better 'ave 'im h'incarcerated!" "Not for worlds, Pelton!" "But it ayn't syfe, to have ä 'uman-tiger, around loose, your ladyship!" "It would be worse, Pelton, to incarcerate him. Think what he would do when he got out!" "Yes?" breathed the horrified Pelton.

"He'd probably tear me limb from limb." "Tear your lady-ship?"— "Limb from limb!" Pelton wiped the beads of perspi-ration from his brow, as this startling picture arose before his throbbing vision. The lady, poised on one leg, like a hurt bird, regarded him gravely. "Don't you see, Pelton, we have to be dip-lomatic! Soothe him; stroke him the right way!" "H'I'd like to stroke him!" muttered Pelton. "Begging your ladyship's pardon, h'I don't believe in soothin'-sirup for 'uman-tigers!" "You think it a waste of good sirup?" "I h'am positive of it." Firmly. "Was your ladyship expecting this person soon?" "Any moment! He's sure to trail me here. Even now, I dare say, he is on my track." Pelton glanced nervously over his shoulder. "H'I'll 'ave the footman, and the gardeners, and MacDuffy, from the stybles! All armed and wyting!" He calls. "We fall upon him! We 'url 'im h'out! And that's the kind of soothin'-sirup I'd recommend."

The lady shook her head. "You don't know Alexander. You might hurl him out but he'd come back." "Not if we fell upon 'im, 'ard enough!" "You'd have to commit murder. And then I'd have to see you all hanged. And that wouldn't do, with the scar-city of servants!" Pelton pondered. "The plan do seem to 'ave its setbacks," he conceded. "All of which brings us back to my way! Be kind, be gentle to him when he comes!" "I could 'ave Tommy, the footman, meet 'im," said Pelton. "Tommy, he do 'ave such a 'eavenly smile! It would melt the 'eart, even, of a 'uman- tiger!" "Yes, I remember. He has a sweet smile," ssented the lady. "Es-pecially, as our American friends would say, after he has had 'a smile,' or two!"

"But who, beggin' your ladyship's pardon, may this 'uman-ti-ger be?" ventured Pelton. "Ah!" said the lady in a thrilling tone. "That is a mystery." "Mystery?" murmured Pelton, with bated breath. "A terrible mystery! He has a hold on me!" "A hold?" "A terrible hold!" The lady clutched the banister. "No; I am not go-ing to fall. I will be brave. I will be calm. Whatever happens, we must be calm. Promise you will be calm, Pelton?" "I—I promise, your ladyship!" "We must humor him." "We—we will." "He will probably ask to see me. You will see that he is permitted to enter." "'Ere?" "Here!" The lady began to limp upward. Near the top she stopped. "Oh, Pelton!" "What, your ladyship?"

"I see him, now!" "Where?" With a violent start. "In my mind's eye! He—he is coming up the hill." "—A 'ill!" "Up! Up!" The lady reached the top of the stairs. "The tea, your ladyship!" The voice was Jane's. The lady turned. "Tea? Ha! While we live, let us drink tea! But first, some dry clothes!"

Chapter VII
Her Ladyship Capitulates

"Here, what you want?" cried James, the JL J-guardian of her ladyship's gates. Alexander, on the point of entering, paused. His manner was lowering. "See that footprint!" he said, pointing. James looked. The imprint of her ladyship's small foot was distinctly discernible on the damp byway. "I follow it," said Alexander. "On the beach —up the hill—to here!" "How dare you follow it?" said the indignant James. "Blarst your impudence!" He got no further. Alexander put out a hand. James went somersaulting into the air and came down in a flower-bed. "Number one!" said a lady, peering from an upper window of the big house. "This promises to be interesting."

Alexander, having disposed of James, strode toward the house. He didn't appear overwhelmed or abashed at its magnificence; on the contrary he seemed hardly to notice how gorgeous it was. Tommy, the footman, met him at the front door. Tommy had received his instructions, and his smile was heavenly; it should have disarmed even a human-tiger. "Ha, ha!" said Tommy. "Oh, my eye! Wouldn't have missed it for anything. It was funny!" "What?" growled Alexander. "Him!" Pointing to James, on the flower-bed. "Oh, my eye! Ha, ha!" "I'll give you an eye!" said Alexander, but he was the least bit disconcerted. By this engaging levity. He had looked for opposition. As he spoke he clenched his mighty fist to carry Out his destructive purpose upon the visage of Tommy when the eye he was planning to smite, winked! And such a wink! A beatific wink! A wink so well calculated to turn away wrath! A wink that seemed to say: "Oh, you couldn't do it, old top! Really now; could you? Think again! Pause; hesitate; reconsider!" Alexander did; that wink bothered him.

He glanced over his shoulder to see if legions were creeping up behind to overwhelm him. Then he wheeled quickly once more upon Tommy. "Where's she?" he said fiercely. "Don't deny she's here, because I trailed her. She tried to give me the slip! Ha, ha!" He gave a blood- curdling laugh. "I'll let her know—" "There! There!" said Tommy, turning a little paler and wondering what Pelton had let him into. "How you do take on! And about nothink, too!" "Nothing!" roared Alexander. "Didn't I tell you, she tried to give me the slip?" "Her ladyship wouldn't have intentionally—" "Cheat me, would she?" Explosively. "I sye! That is going some! You got it wrong, old top; dead wrong!" Soothingly. "W'y, her ladyship wouldn't never dream of cheatin' nobody. W'y, she couldn't. Quite impossible! Arsk the green grocer, or the fish-man, or the wine-merchant. Don't tyke my word!"

"I wouldn't!" said Alexander. "You can't tell me anything about her." Scowling. "I know more about her than you do." "Then," says I, "a blessed privilege has been yours!" Alexander snorted. "Privilege!" "Arsk the tenants! Arsk them, w'at they think of 'er? Anaingel!" Alexander sneered. "Liar!" "I sye!" "Out of my way! I'm coming in!" Again Tommy tried to soothe—to hypnotize; he overworked the heavenly smile. But Alexander seized him by the collar and in another moment Tommy would have followed James into the flower-bed, or the gooseberry bushes, when a soft voice interrupted: "Ah, here you are at last, Alexander! Come right in!"

It was her ladyship. Cordiality was in her mind. She came forward as if welcoming a long- lost friend. "Thomas, did you ask the gentleman in?" Severely. "I—I—" began Thomas. "That will do," said her ladyship, and Thomas, with a consciousness of having failed in what had been expected of him, retired. "I have been expecting you, Alexander," said the lady effusively. "Were you?" Grimly. "Of course!" "I suppose that's why you ran away?" "Ran away! Bless your heart, why should I do that?" Alexander snapped his fingers. "You can't come that over me!" "Of course I knew you would see my footprints and follow." "Oh, you did!" sneered Alexander. "Certainly!"

"Why didn't you wait until I got back?" Roughly. "And have forced you to carry me up-hill? You might have insisted, you know, considering my ankle. No, no; I wished to spare you, and— Welcome to Langlenshire Hall!" Alexander stared. "You aren't going to try to—to have me thrown out?" "What an idea!" Alexander considered. What treachery was her ladyship planning? He gazed cautiously around. "I'll have Pelton show you to your suite," said the lady. "My which?" "Your suite! The king once occupied it, and, in the past, other royal guests have condescended to sleep therein." Alexander searched her face. Was this a trap? Would the royal bed sink into a cellar, or other subterranean depth? Would the top of the bed descend and suffocate him? Alexander had heard of these inhospitable devices.

It might be safer to sleep on the floor. A royal bed had too royal a sound. Those figures in armor, too, standing around, did not look any too reassuring. One of them had a battle-ax swung over the shoulder, and there were lances—what if some one poked a lance through an open window, into him, while he slept? There was quite a lot of money coming to Alexander, and what easier way to get out of paying the same? Alexander made up his mind to sleep with his weather eye open. "Pelton!" The lady was calling to her servitor. Pelton appeared quickly from somewhere. Probably he had been listening close at hand. "Show this gentleman to the blue suite!" commanded her ladyship. "And see that his every want is satisfied. His every want!—Do you understand?" "Ye-es," stammered Pelton. At the same time he could not help wondering what would be the gentleman's "every want."

He looked as if he might call for raw beef. But not Pelton's to reason why. "Follow me, sir," he said in a choked voice. A pretty pass, when a big brigand of the highways, a 'uman-tiger, had to be taken in and housed! Not only to be taken in but to be treated royally, to be pampered and petted and soothed, and to be made much of! Oh, what was his "hold" on her ladyship; what had her ladyship done—what crime committed? It must have been something terrible, to give the 'uman-tiger such a "hold" on her ladyship who, ordinarily, was both high-spirited and in-dependent. Pelton breathed hard. "Follow me,"he said. He did not repeat the "sir." It choked in his throat. Alexander looked at the lady. "How do I know you won't—" he began. "Give you the slip? Well if I did, wouldn't I have to leave you the house?" "Leave 'im the 'ouse!" From Pelton.

"What better guarantee would you ask?" she went on, as Alexander considered. "Would you not find my little obligation amply protected?" "Little obligation!" Pelton thought. Her lady-ship must be frightfully involved. "Surely, the entire estate would cover the indebtednes to you?" she continued. "Entire estate!" Pelton wiped his brow. He so far forgot himself. Alexander hesi-tated. "I guess it's all right," he observed. "But no tricks!" "Great 'eavens! Tricks!" muttered Pelton. "Such langwidge, to 'er lady-ship!" "Here, get a move on you!" said Alexander to Pelton. And Pelton did. But his back bristled, all the way to the royal suite. Had it not been for deserting her ladyship, in time of stress, he would have resigned then and there, for never before had his feelings been so outraged. "See you later!" said Alexander to the lady. And to Pelton the words sounded like a threat.

Chapter VIII
Alexander Makes Himself at Home

Pelton threw open the door leading into the royal suite and, with nose elevated, waited for the visitor to enter. Alexander did so. He walked as if he had been accustomed to royal suites all his days, and to being ushered into them by such superior beings as Pelton. He trod the thick rugs with unconcern; his eyes hardly dwelt upon the beautiful hangings or furniture. He threw himself into a delicate chair that fairly groaned beneath that rough treatment. Pelton threw up his hands. Suppose it broke down? A good hundred guineas gone to smash! Pelton strove to lure. Alexander from the chair. "Here is the bawthroom," he said nervously, throwing open a door. Alexander looked. It was a bathroom fit for Venus. Alexander didn't seem to find it inappropriate for him.

"Humph! Good enough!" he said. Pelton nearly fell over. And this, from a 'uman-tiger! "I'd 'ave you know that the last one of the nobility"—with an accent—"I 'ad the 'onor of h'ushering 'ere, threw up 'er 'ands at the sight of the bathroom, exclaiming—" "Where's the soap?" interrupted Alexander. "Before your h'eyes!" From Pelton, viciously. As he spoke he picked up one of the daintily- covered cakes. "I didn't suppose as 'ow you'd be recognizing of it!" Alexander sniffed. "Got any other kind? I don't like the smell." "Smell! He calls perfume 'smell'! 'Eavenly h'aroma; that's w'at the duchess said it was! And now, to hear h'it called a 'smell'! And by a 'uman-tiger!" "What's that?" said Alexander fiercely. "Nothing!" Hastily. Alexander towered over him. "That last word!"

"H'l was speakin' of h'aromas," said the discomforted Pelton. "We 'as other varieties, h'of course! Try wood violet! I 'ave heard it's göod for the complexion. Or 'eliotrope!" "Bring both," said Alexander in that same menacing tone. "Quite so, sir! I dare say they'll go very well mixed. H'l think you will find h'all the other conveniences, sir." Force of habit would count. Pelton was now sprinkling his effusions with the customary "sirs." "You'll find bawth-robes and dressing-gowns, and is there anything h'else, sir? What about your luggage, sir?" "Haven't got any!" "Bless my soul! A-spendin' a week in a noble 'ouse'old, and without a change of a shirt, not to mention 'is socks! Beggin' your pardon, sir, 'ow do you mean to get on?" "Geton?" Frowning. "Arfter you've 'ad your bawth, and later!"

"W'en you meet 'er ladyship? You h'expect to meet 'er ladyship, don't you? Or, perhaps"— hopefully—"you're not going to stay?" "You bet I'm going to stay!" "Which bein' the case," went on Pelton, feeling himself more hopelessly involved, "'ow are you going to appear for dinner? And do you h'expect to dine with"—desperately— "'er ladyship?" "Dine' with her!" In booming tones. "Of course! That is, I suppose you mean, eat? You bet we eat together. That is"—tapping his chest —"if I want to!" "You!" Pelton's eyes began to pop out again. The visitor's assurance was even more than confusing. Pelton could find no precedent by which to gage it. "Me?" repeated Alexander. "She knows. No woman can tie me to her apron."With an ugly sneer. "Meaning 'er ladyship?" breathed Pelton, eying the visitor with weird fascination.

"Of course!" "Of course!" Weakly from Pelton. The visitor's hold on her ladyship was assuming even more prodigious proportions. Only a murder, committed, could account for it. A murder, committed by her ladyship! Impossible!—and yet— Alas, her ladyship was eccentric. Pelton remembered many artistic conversations over teacups, in the past, wherein her ladyship had professed to yearn for new and outré sensations. Cubic, ultra-impressionistic talk!— Pelton's head went round; something extraordinary had happened. He felt quite incapable of grappling with the situation. "W'ot I was going to say," he murmured weakly, "was, supposin' you do dine with her ladyship, how are you going to do it?" "How? how?" repeated Alexander. "When you eat, you eat!" "But in what?" "Eat in? Of course you eat in. You wouldn't eat out." Alexander was getting angry. What was Pelton doing? Trying to make a monkey of him—Alexander? "W'ot I mean," said Pelton, more helplessly than ever, "is, you 'as to wear somethink, don't you, to eat in?" "You mean my clothes?"

"That's it!" said Pelton. "And look at that shirt!" Despairingly. "And 'im in the royal suite!" "Bah!" exclaimed Alexander ferociously. "I don't mind." "He doesn't mind!" repeated Pelton. "And if I don't mind, it don't matter." "You mean, about w'ot clothes you h'appears in?" "Yes." "At dinner?" "Of course!" "With 'er ladyship?" "Of course!" Pelton clapped his hand to his brow. "H'I'm crazy," he said.

"Only thing you've said that's worth while," remarked Alexander bruskly. "Or, maybe, h'it's only a dream!" Staring at Alexander. "Makes me feel like 'Enery H'lrv- ing. 'Is this a dagger?' Or, 'H'out, vile spot'!" "Meaning me!" "No, no!" Hastily. It was Alexander's turn to stare. "I see where she gets it," he muttered at last. "W'ot?" "It's catching!" "W'ot?" asked Pelton, a second time. "Talking, without saying anything!" Pelton breathed hard. "I'd like to say something," he remarked, with a nasty accent. "I could say something." "I'm waiting," said Alexander. Pelton looked at him, and discretion became the better part of valor. He remembered the reputation her ladyship had given this most unwelcome caller.. "Wot h'l was about to say, was—" He paused. "Was—was—oh, that h'l might be able to find a change of garments for you, sir."

"Ha!" said Alexander. He was not offended. The proffer of old clothes did not cut his proud and haughty spirit. Avarice shone from his eyes. "H'outer and h'inner," went on Pelton. "And some socks which, doubtless, will be h'acceptable, when you 'ave 'ad your bawth!" "Ha! Now you talk sense!" "H'of course, the garments ayn't guaranteed to fit. H'at least, a perfect fit!" "Poof!"said Alexander. He was not concerned about a perfect fit. "And there's shoes!" "Of course!" From Alexander. No old clothes man could have been in a more receptive mood. "Bring plenty! That's as it should be." "H'is h'it?" "Didn't I lose my old duds? And on account of her!" "You did? You and 'er were together?" With awe.

"You bet!" Grinning. "I beg your pardon, sir, this is so extraordinary, but you spoke not long ago as h' if you wouldn't take it h'out of the h'ordinary, dining with 'er ladyship? Am h'l to infer, by h'any chance, you 'as ever ate with 'er ladyship?" "Bah!"said Alexander. "We ate from the same sausage!" "Good heavings!" murmured Pelton. "A Langlenshire, and 'im, from the same sausage!" "Yes, I gave her a piece," said Alexander virtuously. "I always believe in treating them well." "In treating 'er well!"from the stupefied Pel-ton. "That is," added Alexander, "when they behave!" "Behave! 'Er, behave! To 'im!" "It was a fine sausage, too! A first-class sausage!" "Heaven be praised it were first-class!" "I could have eaten it all, too." ruminated Alexander, a faint regret in his tone.

"I can still eat. When you go for the duds you might tell her to bring me something to eat." "Tell 'er —to bring you "— "Can't you hear?"Fiercely. "I don't think h'I can!"Feebly. "Tell 'er —" "Bah! Hasn't she waited on me before, and carried bundles." "Bundles! 'Er!" "Old duds!" "Meanin' old clothes?" "Sure! Old clothes! Mine!" "Yours?" "Mine!" "'Er, carryin' your—" But it was too much. Further comment along this line failed Pelton. He shook his head. "Help yourself," he said with a vague gesture. "I will," said Alexander. Pelton looked at him as if he saw him at a great distance. "Kings has washed theirselves in there,"he said, looking toward the bathroom.

"Tub's pretty small," said Alexander with a curl of the lip. "Kings has bore with h'it!" "Well, wishing won't make it bigger." "It won't." Then Pelton walked toward the door; he could still walk. He was thankful for that. This visitor had a very benumbing effect on him. He managed to stagger out. A short time later Alexander was splashing in the tub.

CHAPTER IX
FINE FEATHERS

"May I enter?" asked her ladyship, gazing toward the closed door at the far end of the royal suite. As she spoke she held herself poised nervously; she had not closed the door leading out into the hall from the sitting-room, where she now stood. She wished, no doubt, to leave the way open for a quick and precipitate retreat, should the occasion or necessity arise for such action on her part. One couldn't depend upon Alexander. - He was an unknown quantity—such a simple child of nature! "Why do you say 'May I come in?' when you have?" rumbled a powerful masculine voice from the royal bathroom, in answer to her ladyship's somewhat timid inquiry. "The question does seem superfluous," assented the lady. "But"—apologetically— "I knocked and you did not hear.

So I took the liberty—shall I say, the very great liberty?—of entering." "Be out in a moment!" called Alexander. And he was. The lady started violently. Her heart had pounded; then, subsided. There was no occasion for alarm. She could regard Alexander calmly—not to say admiringly. He was arrayed in a dressing-gown of gorgeous Chinese pattern. He gleamed and glistened with butterflies and dragons. He was resplendent as a Mogul emperor. All he needed was the Temple of Heaven to complete the illusion. "Oh!" said the lady. This gorgeous vision! —this new Alexander!—this great, big exotic butterfly! It was too overwhelming! "Pelton told me you wished something to eat, and I was to serve you," she murmured humbly. "Yes," said Alexander absently, occupied with his own reflection in a long mirror. He hardly looked at the lady. The latter smiled.

She was recalling certain vague apprehensions of a few moments before. How needless they had been! Alexander in a mood to bestow upon her unwelcome attentions? Alexander, a possible

40

cave man? It "was to laugh." His mood was, essentially, non-am-atory. Or, if he was in love, she knew with whom it was. No such poor, little, insignificant object as herself! Alexander was in love with a big magnificent male-man. He was an amplified Narcis-sus! He could stand for hours and contemplate his own reflec-tion. My! but he made her feel insignificant. "Pelton told me you were hungry," she said in that same humble tone. "I am!" Still looking at himself. "I brought up a pork pie and beer." Alexander condescended to turn—to look at her—or the beer! "Give it to me!" He was referring to the beer. Meekly she obeyed. He raised the pitcher to his lips. "Here is a glass."

"What I want that for?" Alexander drank from the pitcher. "Ha!" he said, wiping his lips. "Meaning: 'Good'?" "You bet." "I am pleased"—she began demurely. "More!" interrupted Alexan-der. His tone was brusk —peremptory. It awoke a little spark in the lady's breast. A butterfly may be a butterfly, but a worm is also a worm. From time immemorial it has been privileged to turn. Her ladyship rang for Jane. There was a limit to this personal ser-vice business, even if you did happen to be married to the object of it. "More, indeed!" she remarked. "Your name ought to be Oliver. And drinking out of the pitcher! What will the servants think?" Alexander did not answer. He was too busy, strutting! His self-adulation began to get on the lady's nerves. "I suppose you think I ought to be proud to wait on you?—to fetch and carry?—to bring you beer?—to serve your every whim?"

"Proud?" said Alexander absently. "Such a magnificent spec-imen! I suppose I should get down on my knees before you!" "If you want!" From Alexander. "I don't care." "No?" The lady caught her breath. "You have but one concern." Looking at the reflec-tion. As she spoke she clasped her hands mockingly. "Do let me worship you, from a distance!" "If you like!" In that same tone. "Thanks! I—" "Where's the beer?" "Beer?" She caught her breath. "I ask permission to worship and he answers: 'Beer'!" "Didn't I tell you to get more?" Accusingly. "I believe you did." With rising breast. "Well?" Sternly. "I told Jane to get it!" "Jane?"Alexander looked at her. "'But why?" "I am still just a little lame!" Alexander's face changed slightly. "Not much! Besides, it is hard to tear myself from your presence. Can you not understand that? You who are so—so— what shall I call it? Not beautiful!" "Grand," suggested Alexander modestly.

"Yes; that's it. You do forgive me for sending Jane under the circumstances, that I may obey that impulse to tarry here and gaze?" "You poke fun?" asked Alexander suspiciously. "Fun! He calls these love-pangs fun!" "You don't feel well?" "What do you care? Narcissus!" "Is that, pet-name?" "It is the name of a man who was turned into a tree." "A tree?" "Yes. For despising our poor sex! As you do!" "Me?" "Don't you?" "Not all!" Gallantly. "There was dish-washer once—big, pot-washing woman"—he opened his arms—"Whew!"

"Why do you say: 'Whew'?" "What you have me say?" "I?" Haughtily. "She fine big woman," said Alexander with tender reminiscences in his tone. "A pot-washer preferred to me!" A peal of merriment rang from the lady's lips. And then she obeyed one of those aberrant impulses that sometimes swept over her. Her little hand swept out; it caught the grinning, boastful Alexander fair on the cheek. Smack! Not a ladylike performance? Anyhow, the lady felt better. Almost at once. She smiled divinely. "Oh, my poor Alexander! Did I hurt you?" she cooed. Alexander rubbed the spot. The uncouth grin had forsaken his features. The arms he had extended as if embracing a barrel, fell to his side. "Oh, oh! Such a shocking temper!" she murmured. "All the Langlenshires have shocking tempers. They're so high-bred, you see. You must make allowances, dear, dear Alexander!"

Alexander continued to rub. "Am I dreaming?" said his expression. "I shall never forgive myself," murmured the lady. "You!" Suddenly he turned, a rumbling sound in his throat. So a mighty beast might roar before it leapt upon its prey. Did he expect to see the lady run? To flee for her life? If so, Alexander was doomed to disappointment. It is true she became paler, but she stood her ground. Not only that, she looked the 'uman-tiger in the eye—proudly, fearlessly. So a high-bred Langlenshire lady had once looked the executioner in the eye, in the dim and distant past, and gone proudly to her doom. That look held Alexander, for a second. "You know, I can break you in two?" he growled. "It is possible." Tranquilly. "Or toss you up to the ceiling?" "Also, 'no doubt!" "Or out of the window?" "Presumably incontrovertible!"

"You, not afraid?" "I am afraid not." "Of being thrown out of the window?" "I have always wanted to fly. It has been my childhood dream." Alexander sighed. What are you going to do with a wife like that? Preconceived notions disintegrated. She wasn't afraid of him or anything. "You not afraid of being beaten?" "Try it and see!" With a smile. "You wouldn't mind?" Still puzzled. "Why should I, if it gave you pleasure?"she said softly. "That sounds all right," said Alexander dubiously. "You do what I say, and you won't catch it!" "You will find me a regular Griselle." "Who she?" "A lady who always minded her husband." "I like to know her."

"But you can't. She lived about five hundred years ago." "Humph!" said Alexander. "Not many of them left!" "Say not so!" "My wife obey! You bet." "But there are few men like you!" Dotingly. "Yes. Lots of women look at me." "Can you blame them?" "Bah! I don't let them bother me." "What a relief to hear you say that!" "I look at them if I want to, though!" said Alexander. "Let me catch you!" Half-hysterically. "You think I'm only for you?" "I did have some such notion." "Huh!" said Alexander. Such an immoral "Huh!" She was so glad Pelton didn't hear him; or the curate! "You go see about that beer," said Alexander. "Why it doesn't come!"

"That odious word again. Beer!" "I like it foamy, and bigger pitcher!" A moment the lady looked at him. Words seemed about to leap from her lips, but they didn't. Instead, she smiled queerly.

"Shall I take your boots and have them blacked?" "Yes; take 'em away," said Alexander. "But don't forget to bring 'em back!" "I'll try not to!" murmured the lady, and picked up the mighty boots in her small hands. "If there is anything else, call me!" "I will. You bet," said Alexander, and tackled the pork pie.

"My eye! did you see that?" said Tommy to Pelton, whom he met coming up-stairs with an armful of old clothes, "'Er ladyship, with 'is boots!" "Did I see h'it?" Pelton groaned. "'Ave I lived to see h'it, you should be arsking. W'ot a hold 'e must 'ave on 'er! But hurry arfter 'er, Tommy." "For why?" "It wouldn't surprise me, h'if 'er ladyship shined 'em h'up, with 'er own delicate 'igh-bred 'ands!" "My eye!"said Tommy. And then: "Did you hear that?" "I did." Peering down. "She dropped 'em! Over the banisters! And Jane 'as them!" "She ayn't going to brush them 'erself, 'eaven be praised!" said Pelton. "Amen!" said Tommy.

CHAPTER X
THE MONSTER AND THE ARTIST

"Who are you?" said Alexander, staring at the intruder. "I am, monsieur, the valet?" "Valley, eh?" Alexander, still in the butterfly gown, stood surrounded by old clothes that looked new to him. This little "double-radish of a man" had blown in after Pelton, with the old duds. He danced around vivaciously and seemed trying to give a good impression. Pelton, himself, had hurriedly retreated after having brought the old garments. Alexander looked while the little man spread out this garment and that. He hopped from trousers, to waistcoat, and then, with birdlike agility, hopped from neckties to collars and shirts, laying them out on chairs and settees, and springing back and forth, to contemplate the general effect, from different angles. And while thus contemplating the visitor, Alexander's gaze seemed to say:"Why is it? And why has Pelton wished it on me? Where did it come from? And will it hop out of the window next?" "Monsieur can address me as Jacques," observed the little man, in cheery tones that seemed to fit the birdlike motions. "Jack!" rumbled Alexander. "Jumping-Jack, I should say!" "As monsieur pleases," said the little man amiably. "I think ze garments, zey fit monsieur. I find zem in ze discard." "Look like new to me!" "Zey belong to male relative of her ladyship. He leave them behind. We resurrect for monsieur. I sponge out ze shine. But I hear monsieur has suffered ze shipwreck? Zat all hees magnifique wardrobe, eet is lost?" "Magni f— What?"

"Ze half-dozen trunks, with ze priceless wardrobe of monsieur — Ze cruel waves have engulfed zem?" "Who's been talking?" growled Alexander. "Her ladyship. She tell Jane." "Oh!" said Alexander. He would be prepared for anything now. "Ze ship, he sink, suddenly! Monsieur, he grab ze first clothes—a sailor's! And so, he come ashore!" "Humph!" growled Alexander.

45

His wife's imagination was paralyzing to him sometimes. "Hear anything else?" "Nossing! But ze cook, she say her ladyship hint at a great, a very great secret!" Alexander pondered. What new and subtle treachery was her ladyship planning? Apparently he had dropped into the very lap of luxury. All the gifts of the gods were his for the asking. Gifts! Ha! When Greeks come bearing gifts, look out! So ran the old saying. Why should it apply only to Greeks?

Alexander regarded the old clothes. Gifts! Heaps of them! This fair daughter of the North was a veritable goddess of plenty. Look out for her! Alexander regarded the jumping-jack, her minion, suspiciously. "If monsieur will recline in ze big chair, I will bestow upon· monsieur ze shave!" "Give me a shave, eh?" said Alexander. Suppose Jacques should cut his throat? Would her ladyship proceed to such an extremity? Alexander knew of people along the water-fronts of his native land, who had cut throats for less than was at stake in this instance. He knew of one sanguinary transaction that had involved only about a sixpence— Now her ladyship was indebted to Alexander for about three thousand— Jacques prepared his razors. Alexander watched. The little man's expression was blithe and inoffensive; he seemed as cheerful as a Mozart Allegro. He hummed a gay air, as he tested a sharp edge with his finger. Alexander decided to trust him. He sat down and elevated his chin.

Jacques shaved him with little angel touches. Alexander could hardly feel them. "When are you going to begin?" growled Alexander. "I have begun. I have ze one cheek all finished." Alexander felt something like a rose-leaf brushing his other cheek. "Here, don't tickle!" "Eet is ze razaire, monsieur." "Razor?" said Alexander. His idea of a razor was something that ripped and tore—at least, of something you were aware of! "I don't hardly feel it." "Oh, monsieur, I am ze artiste, not ze butch- aire!" "Hope you'll know when you've got it done!" said Alexander. "I wouldn't!" "Monsieur is not pleased?" "Well, when I get shaved I like to know it." Jacques hippety-hopped about some more; flicked and fluttered with his fingers, and then announced with the pride of a master :

"Eet is finished!" "Where's the perfume?" demanded Alexander. "I have already a very delicate essence applied, monsieur." "Can't smell it!" "Oh, monsieur, eet is not, zee what you call pronounced smell. Eet is aristocratic perfume— of ze bon-ton!" "Gimme, me something you can smell!" Jacques made a despairing gesture. "What's that big bottle of stuff in there?" demanded Alexander, pointing to the bathroom. "Zat, monsieur, is ze powerful cologne we have use, some time ago, when a rat, he die in ze wall." "Ha, ha!"roared Alexander. "He very aristocratic rat; he die in wall of royal suite. Mon Dieu! perhaps he royal rat, but he smell just like common rat. Oh, ze terrible aroma! I rush to ze pharmacy. I call for ze strongest perfume. 'Give me ze perfume zat drown ze dead-rat aroma,' I call for. Zey give me zat. I sprinkle near ze grave of ze rat, but I know not which— Mon Dieu! —is ze worse"— "Go bring it!" Jacques obeyed. Alexander poured some in his hands.

Then he sniffed. "That's something like," he said, and applied the same. "Now I know I've had a shave!" Jacques drooped. Also he sniffed. "Alas, monsieur, eet revive zee memory of zee sad obsequies!" "None of your woman's perfume for me!" said Alexander, getting up and surveying himself once more in the long mirror. "And speaking of women—any good-looking women down in the servants' quarters?" he asked. As he spoke, he winked. What he intended to imply was that few women could resist that combination of him (Alexander) and the perfume. Alexander had been almost irresistible before, but now—his leer was devastating. "Oh, monsieur!" cried the shocked Jacques. "Monsieur would not look in the servants' quarters. He would turn up hees nose at zee women zare."

"Wait till I have a look at 'em!" said Alexander. Jacques leaned against the wall. "A monstaire!—a devastating monstaire!"

he thought. Pelton had been right. A 'uman-tiger, that's what the visitor was. And now he was getting ready to devastate the servants' quarters! A shiver ran down Jacques' back. The sweet Marguerite—the laundress—and the idol of Jacques' heart!—would she be sacrificed to this insatiable monster—this Minotaur? "Zee women, in zee servants' quarters, zey are all hideous," murmured Jacques. "Then I won't waste my time," said Alexander. "Unless they're big like this—"He put out his arms. Jacques' heart leaped hopefully. His sweetheart was petite—the littlest creature. He began to skip around once more. Not his to worry about Cook, a three-hundred-pounder—

"And now, if monsieur would kindly discard zee gorgeous dressing-gown?" "Take this off!" "How can monsieur dress for zee dinnaire unless he discard him?" asked Jacques blithely. Alexander heaved a sigh; likewise, he heaved off his beautiful butterfly robe. As he stood in the new-found union suit Pelton had managed to provide, Jacques chirped with new approval. Never had he valetted for a finer put-up gentleman!—or monster. True, he was terrifically odorous, but that, after all, was a matter of taste. If he preferred to reek with that antidote to lifeless-rodent aroma, was it not his own concern? Jacques was a true Frenchman in his belief in the personal-liberty idea. Every one to his taste! Monsieur was a free agent. So Jacques adjusted a stiff white shirt upon Alexander and held the trousers for him to wedge into. A quarter of an hour or so, and a different Alexander walked up and down. His face showed approval. That butterfly gown was beautiful, no doubt, and becoming to him; but this garb, too, had its advantages.

It "showed off" Alexander's superb athletic contours. In that other garb, one looked more at the butterflies. "My, what fine shoes!" True, they pinched Alexander's toes, but what mattered that? They were so shiny. One could gaze and gaze at them. Alexander did. He stuck out his feet and surveyed them from different angles. He was thus agreeably occupied when Pelton again looked in. "Dinner is served, sir!" "Dinner?" Alexander had, shortly before, demolished a pork-pie, but he displayed marked interest in Pelton's announcement. "Where do I eat?" "He will lead the way," said Pelton haughtily. And then, as if to explain his own condescension: "'Er ladyship's orders!"

Chapter XI
Prestidigation

Pelton ushered Alexander into the library, the former apparently suffering, en route, for he sniffed hard and breathed harder. "Great 'eavens! w'ot h'am I a-usherin' into 'er ladyship's presence!" Her ladyship, reclining in a large chair, looked up at Alexander's entrance. 'Oh, what a charming fragrance!" she observed languidly. "Charming!" Pelton nearly exploded, but managed, somehow, to efface himself. "Mad! Stark mad!" he confided to Jane. "'Ere he comes down, smellin' like a pestilence, and her elevates her delicate nostrils and says: "'Ow charmin'!"

"Not mad, I call it," answered Jane. "I has my theory. Once I saw a play, and in it a lady falls in love with a donkey, and she acted that foolish, a-ticklin' of 'is long ears, I could 'ardly hold in. But she couldn't 'elp it, poor thing, 'cause she'd had a love-potion. My theory is: He's give her a love-potion." "Bless my 'eart!" cried the startled Pelton. "And she can't help -lovin' him! That's the secret of the 'old he has on her." But Pelton shook his head. "H'I'm stickin' to the crime theory!" Meanwhile, her ladyship, in the library, was examining Alexander with a critical and astonished eye. "Stand still!" Alexander obeyed. "Wonderful!" said the lady. Alexander held himself with the ease of one to the manner born. He even shoved a hand negligently in his trousers pocket and leaned with careless grace against the mantel.

"Wonderful!" repeated the lady once more. "Don't move." Alexander found pleasure in obeying. "I could never have believed it!" Then she heaved a sigh. "A perfect prototype of one of De Maurier's perfect masculine drawing-room creations!" Alexander shifted to a new posture of grace, leaning the other arm against the mantel and shoving the other hand in his trousers pocket. "Well, of course, I'll believe anything after this," she murmured. "What a pity the illusion will have to be dispelled." "What's that?" said Alexander. As he spoke, he moved partly across the room. The lady noticed his stride (tight shoes!) was no longer bold and devastating. He didn't knock over any chairs, or upset and ruin priceless vases. He negotiated the distance between the mantel and the table safely. Having progressed thus far, Alexander leaned with one hand on the table and the other on his hip.

Another perfect De Maurier hero-pose! To continue to regard Alexander was almost as good pastime as turning the pages of an old, and eminently respectable, volume of Punch. Alexander not only did not outwardly offend; he was a positive artistic pleasure. "What was I saying?" murmured the lady. "Oh, something about illusions being dispelled later! I was thinking of dinner."She might have added:And the manner in which he would eat it! But she didn't. Sufficient unto the moment, etc. Why disturb the perfect spell of the moment? Why not enjoy Alexander——though briefly—when one could? Let Pelton wait, out there, in the dining-room! Let the soup get a bit cold! Discipline had been thrown to the winds anyhow. "How do you like my gown?" she asked of Alexander. He contemplated her. It was a "dream," and the lady's perfect shoulders and arms completed a dazzling picture.

"All right!" he said. Perfect nonchalance! No true Britisher could have surveyed that enticing vision with greater lethargy. In the presence of attractions like unto those of Hebe, Alexander seemed to suffer from coma or a stroke of mental paralysis. What could have been more perfectly high-bred? The lady clapped her hands. "Wonderful!" she said for the third time. And Alexander didn't even ask what was wonderful. He didn't seem to care. Absence of curiosity! How his virtues were piling up! What the lady had previously considered stupidity and ignorance, she now discovered to be insouciance. Insouciance!—Yes, that was it. Alexander (dressed up!) had the most perfect insouciance in the world. "Too bad!" she murmured. "But I suppose we'll have to go in! If we don't, Pelton will probably give me notice." As she

spoke she arose. Alexander, divining her action was the signal
that they were to eat, negotiated his way, without mishap, to the
dining-room door.

He didn't enter the room first, either. Perhaps his shoes had
begun to pinch worse than ever and therefore his progress was
retarded? Or, possibly, her ladyship walked a little more quickly
than was her wont. Be that as it may, she reached the threshold
first and so was enabled to enter the room ahead of Alexander. If
the latter noted this remissness, or want of manners, on her part,
he did not speak of it, or reprove her. Perhaps he was considering,
more primarily, a tureen of steaming soup which refreshed his
vision as he stepped into the noble banqueting-room. A servant
had but removed the lid, and the massive proportions of the bowl
were reassuring. The lady did not intend to starve him, whatever
dire plans and conspiracies were brewing in her brain. Pelton
looked after the lady's chair and Alexander sauntered—with insouciance—to his place. He couldn't have done it better, if he
had rehearsed for months.

He didn't seem overwhelmed at the sight of rare china and
massive silver plate, though his eye did rove toward the soup. But
even the most impervious of men may display a passing interest
in soup, though they may regard their beautiful hostess as but
a species of china doll. The lady noticed the glance and did not
disapprove. She beamed on Alexander. Even Pelton, she concluded, would have to be impressed by that insouciance. And then, a
sudden dread assailed her. All this was too good to last. Why had
she not thought, in time, to have the soup cut out? Alexander
looked slightly surprised when he saw Pelton serve her ladyship
first. The lady imagined it was on the point of his tongue to
expostulate, but, fortunately, before his slow brain had time to
formulate an expression of protest, Pelton had placed the soup
before Alexander. The latter grasped the spoon. The lady shuddered. Alexander looked at her.

For a moment he watched how she dipped, and sipped noiselessly. "Haw! haw!" he laughed. Then a whimsical fancy seemed to seize him. That must be mighty hard to do. Any one could devour soup, the while making sounds like a suction-pump in action, but noiselessly to dispose of it?——Perhaps her ladyship thought she was the only one in the world who could do that? Perhaps she was trying "to put one over" on Alexander? Perhaps she was endeavoring to demonstrate her own superiority, as a table-prestidigitator? Her manner was very severe and superior. "Ha! ha!" laughed Alexander again. He couldn't do that, eh? He would show her! He could do some tricks, himself. So he did what she did. Some spoon-juggler, eh? Just as gently; not a splash; not a sound; silence like the stillness of a graveyard! Again, ha! ha! an inner, ha! ha! One had to have a steady hand and good nerves! Well, that meant him, Alexander!

He didn't spill a drop. Superb; magnificent! He leaned back triumphantly. Try to "put one over" on him, would she? The lady's face was a study. Alexander had fathomed her thoughts; she divined the reason for his triumph. What an intuition he possessed; what a positively uncanny brain! Why, he could read people! Amazing! The lady was beginning to feel a bit bewildered with her paragon. She felt he might be getting slightly beyond her. This was not flattering to her own pride. But she had to conceal her own feelings. She laughed. Pelton would think they were both laughing at some funny joke, perhaps, that had been exchanged between them in the library. "Tell me something else funny," said the lady, for Pelton's ears. "Humph!" said Alexander. And the lady laughed, as if that was funny! "I say"—Alexander looked over his shoulder. The soup-tureen had disappeared. More soup was written in his eyes.

"Did you speak, sir? Yes, sir?" From Pelton. "The gentleman was about to ask for wine, Pelton," interposed the lady quickly. Alexander was about to expostulate, but he didn't. Soup was all right but wine was better. "Yes, bring the wine." "Young, or heavy?" said the lady. "Heavy," said Alexander. "The best, Pelton!"

said the lady. "Of course!" put in Alexander. Pelton choked. This 'uman-tiger wanted to be fed high. The "best" was none too good for him! Had Jane been right, after all, about the love- potion? The rest of the repast seemed, to the lady, like a dream. Alexander continued to demonstrate for her benefit that he, too, was a prestidigitator. He elevated three peas dexterously on a silver fork, when he could have shoveled in a dozen with his knife. If she could do it, he could. He could do anything any woman could, was his attitude.

He performed untold prodigies of skill. He watched the lady and picked out the right piece of silverware. His precision, in this respect, almost caused the lady to expire with astonishment. The deliberation with which he started the attack on each course, would be attributed, of course, by the observant Pelton, to the guest's naturally slow and phlegmatic disposition. The lady started to giggle. She couldn't help it. When Alexander reached, without one single mistake, the ice-cream spoon, the humor of the situation so tickled her funny-bone that she simply had to laugh and laugh. Pelton had, never before, seen her so merry. He switched, more strongly, to Jane's theory. It might be love-potion working. What would her ladyship do next? Peals of silvery merriment shocked the atmosphere of that staid and respectable old place. "I have so enjoyed this dinner!" Pelton tried hard not to blush for her ladyship. The love-potion must have been a powerful one. Pelton modestly hoped he would be able to get away from the room without being shocked to a still greater degree.

"Never have I been more entertained!" the lady went on. "H'entertained?" thought Pelton. "H'and 'im, hardly say in' of a word, and h'only h'openin' his mouth to put somethink in h'it!" And yet her ladyship's eyes shone as if she had been listening- to all manner of witty sayings! She seemed as gay as if Alexander were a light comedian, or gentleman of the old school with a fund of anecdotes at his tongue's end. "You may leave the cigars and cigarettes, Pelton," said the lady. Pelton was but too pleased to get away. His exit was unusually forceful and dignified. The lady turned to Alexander. "How nice!" she said in her sprightliest. "To be alone, at last!" "Is it?" said Alexander. "Do light one," she said, pressing on him the cigars. Alexander did, and soon began blowing vast clouds around him.

The fragrance of cigar drowned that other antidote-to-dead-rodent-in- the-wall aroma. The lady studied him. "You are very apt at learning!" "Eh?" She repeated the remark. "You mean—I got brains?" said Alexander. "I wonder?" "Oh, I got brains all right!" said Alexander simply, if not over-modestly. "I show you!" "You have! You did!" There was a faint look of inquiry in the lady's eyes; she blew rings that mingled with the denser smoke from Alexander's cigar. Then suddenly she arose. "Shall we go into the billiard-room?" And Alexander followed insouciantly.

CHAPTER XII
A GOOD SPORT

The lady held her head higher, and told herself she would, at any rate, enjoy beating Alexander at billiards. She played unusually well, and was quite confident of her skill. And she did beat Alexander—badly! Her expectations, in this respect, were fully realized. Alexander played about as she imagined he would. With much vigor—sans skill! He sought to accomplish by sheer strength what science alone could accomplish. Even when the balls began flying from the table, and she had to dodge, the lady acted as if she were having "the time of her life." She scored and Alexander perspired. He did little else. He might imitate her dining-room table-prestidigitation, but here was a quality of juggling not so easily copied.

That blind expenditure of brute strength afforded the lady the opportunity she desired. She breathed a little homily on intelligence versus mere forcible physical effort! She waxed quite philosophical, and, incidentally, deliciously ironical. She punctured the animal and his pretenses with deft and delightful abandon. Alexander began to glare. He was beginning to get angry; no doubt about that! He tossed his head like a bull in the ring:—a bull that has expended a lot of effort without tangible results. "Take it easier!" said the lady, with a mocking smile, as a red ball hopped from the table and went skipping down the room, with the exasperated Alexander in hot pursuit. Alexander muttered something; the ball evaded his clumsy hands and he bumped his head. The lady leaned back and laughed and laughed; then she delivered another homily. Alexander glared some more, which pleased the lady.

"Good!" Triumphantly. "Where's your insular calm now? And so it was all a fraud and a sham, after all?" "I take it easier next time," said Alexander through his teeth. "I surprise you!" Next time, however, fate arranged an almost impossible shot. "Ha, ha!" said the lady. "Poor Alexander! Only an expert could make that one. I doubt if I could do it. In fact, I'm sure I couldn't!" "I make him," said Alexander violently. "Indeed?"she breathed mockingly. "What you bet I don't make him?" demanded Alexander angrily. "Bet? Another British trait! Ha, ha! The making of a sport in you!" "What you bet?" he persisted, even more violently. "Well, if you win, you may—kiss my hand! I dare risk such a reward because there is not the slightest chance of your performing the impossible."

"Make it two pounds," said Alexander practically. "How dare you!" said the lady with flashing eyes. "You make it two pounds, I can't do it?" reiterated Alexander. "There are men," said the lady haughtily, "who would prefer the other alternative to two hundred pounds!" "I, kiss your hand? That gets me nowhere," said Alexander. "But with two pounds—" "Say no more!" said the lady, with a proud toss of the Langlenshire head. "Two pounds it shall be!" Alexander surveyed the balls carefully. "I play very careful," he said. "Maybe I make him! I watch you. I play like you, now!" The cue now became a delicate thing in his hands; he poised it most lightly and calculated with much care and apparent concentration. Then he paused, once more, to look up at the lady. "I make him!"

"Why don't you?" she responded ironically. The cue shot forth. Alexander began to register exultation. "You see, what happen! I know how to play, now. I make him!" And he did. Alexander had accomplished the almost impossible. The lady looked; and then she regarded Alexander. There was a frown on her face and a question in her deep eyes. "Was it accident?" she said, as if to herself. "I study; I see how you do it," said Alexander. "Me study how you do juggle-tricks with all kinds of funny table-silver. I, too, can do! And here, too! What you can do, I can do!" He tapped his chest—an abominable habit! "I should call you a star pupil, Alexander," said the lady quietly. "And if I did not have every confidence in your absolute integrity, I might be capable of thinking you had been, what our American friends call 'stringing me'! For the ignoble purpose of adding two vulgar pounds to your constantly growing earthly possessions! Shall we go on with our game?"

"We bet some more?" Quickly. "No, Alexander! I cast no aspersion on your probity of character, but we bet no more!" "You, no good sport?" "I am beginning to wonder if it would be sport?" said the lady. "Would I stand a sporting chance?" "Didn't I make some pretty bum playing?" demanded Alexander. "You did! But you have improved so fast, the teacher now wonders if she has become the pupil? May I sit at your feet?" "All right! We play for nothing," said Alexander. And once more the balls began to fly off the table with the seemingly very much annoyed Alexander in hot pursuit. "I think that will be sufficient," said the lady quietly, after this performance had been repeated a few times. Then she yawned. "I fear me, you are deeper than I thought. I imagined I had delved into you, Alexander, but I have just skimmed the surface of the ocean?"

"What you mean?" "That it is getting late and time to retire! Do you think you can find your way to the royal suite?" "You bet!" "I trust you will find the bed comfortable, Alexander." "I ring for another if it isn't." "Oh, yes!" With rising inflection. "So you could!" "I like lots of room for kicking!" "Well, if you find the royal bed too short, just tell Pelton to lengthen it. Don't be afraid of making trouble!" "I won't! I make him hop!" "If he should prove ineffectual, you might call the rest of the household." "That bully good idea." The lady's sarcasm was lost on Alexander. "You bet! I make 'em all hop!" "If necessary, you could summon me!" That should have overwhelmed Alexander, but did it?

"You bet!" he said. "I make you hop, too!" Her breast arose. "Would you change us all into—hoppers? Would you invite a veritable plague of locusts?—a famine on the neighborhood? Spare us, Alexander! Spare—", She clasped her hands. "These shoes too blamed tight to stop for nonsense talk!" said Alexander. "You wish larger ones?" He considered. "Maybe I like small feet, too. I look fine with small feet." "Oh, vanity!"she breathed, and then: "Good night!" She extended her hand. Under the circumstances, she felt she ought, at least, do that. Especially when he was the occupant of the royal suite! Alexander vouchsafed to take the hand. One has to be diplomatic with people who owe you money. Their fingers touched, but no more! In shuffling about the billiard-table, chasing balls, Alexander seemed to have fairly surcharged his body with electricity, for when the lady's hand came in contact with his, there was a definite shock and spark.

It was as if her ladyship had touched a small battery. "Oh!" "Haw! haw!" laughed Alexander. "Funny way to shake hands! Eh?" "I do not find it—funny!" "Let's try it again!" said Alexander, just as if he were playing a game. "Thank you, I decline!" "All right!" Alexander turned. "Pigs' feet goes well for dinner, sometimes!" "I'll—I'll speak to the cook.' "With noodles!" "You—you shall have them." "I don't like—if you forget Suspiciously. "Forget anything that appeals to you? Never!" "Humph!" said Alexander. The lady watched him go, "What—what a positively wifely feeling that man inspires in me!" she thought.

Chapter XIII
High Morality

But her ladyship's cares were not over for the day. At the door
of her suite—on the other side of the house from the royal apartments, occupied by Alexander!—she found a small delegation
awaiting her. There was Pelton, Tommy, James, Jane, the cook,
and others, including, even, the vivacious Jacques. Nervousness
or embarrassment, mixed with determination, was depicted on
their faces. The lady glanced at them all casually. "Come to say
good night? So good of you, I am sure!" "We 'asn't come exactly
for that, your ladyship," said the embarrassed Pelton. "No?"Vivaciously.

"No!" Faintly. "Go on!" said the voice of Jane, as Pelton hesitated and swallowed. "Don't be hurryin' of him!" said Tommy.
"Him acts as if him was afraid!" From Jane. "What of?" From her
ladyship. "I hope you haven't been doing anything you shouldn't,
Pelton!" "H'l?" stammered Pelton. "H'it ayn't me—"Again he
paused. "The truth is, your ladyship, we 'as 'ad a meeting." "We?"
"All your ladyship's 'elp! That is, h'all except Bobby MacDuffy,
the styble-man, who, being a h'atheist, said as 'ow it wasn't any of
'is business!" "What?" "'Igh h'English morality!" "I do say as how
bishops is humbugs!" From Jane, horrified. "And it is to complain
of MacDuffy that you are come to interview me? I have nothing
to do with his private opinions. And he has a perfect right to his
opinion of bishops." "H'it wasn't to complain of 'im that we are
'ere," said Pelton. "H'it"— "Well?" "Go on!" From Jane. Pelton
seemed to find difficulty in doing so. "You have come to complain of some one?" said her ladyship. "We 'as!" Weakly. "Well?"
"Say w'at you said down there," urged Tommy. "Where we had
the meeting!" "I spoke up then, all right enough!" From Jane. "So
loud and 'ighly respectable! It were like preaching." "Yes, Pelton,
say what you said down there," said her ladyship, with a sweet

60

smile. "You all assembled, and—" "There was some talk,"went on Pelton, thus encouraged, "each expressin' 'is or 'er mind, in a 'ighly respectful manner toward your ladyship, exceptin' MacDuffy, who wasn't there—" "Leave'im out" From Tommy.

"Get on," said Jane. "I is," said Pelton miserably. "He calls that getting on!" From Jane. "And him the spokesman!" "Tell it yourself," said Pelton. "Yes, Jane?" said her ladyship. "It's your ladyship's conduct!" said Jane in an awful tone. "My—what?" "Conduct!" "And you have called to complain of that? Is that all?" Brightly. "Oh, dear, I thought it was something serious." "Ayn't it serious, your ladyship?" From Pelton. "Dear me, no! Some one has always been complaining of my conduct. You have no idea how often my uncle, the lord high chancellor, has taken me to task for doing something unconventional, shall we call it?" "That might do," said Pelton. "It would be a way of describing it, your ladyship," said Jane. "You mean, a polite way!" Jane had the grace to blush. "H'it wouldn't be as h'if we weren't old, old servants!" went on Pelton plaintively. "W'ot 'as always 'ad your ladyship's welfare at 'eart! W'ot 'as always looked up to your ladyship, as all that was 'igh, and 'ighly respectable! It wouldn't be as if some of us 'adn't known your ladyship w'en she was a 'igh-bred, 'ighly respectable h'infant in arms!" "I understand," said her ladyship, deeply touched. "And I trust I am not ungrateful for your combined moral solicitude." "Put it to her ladyship so as not to hurt her feelin's! Them were his instructions at the meeting," said Tommy. In the background, Cook began to snivel. Cook was sensitive and easily affected. Her two or three hundred pounds avoirdupois concealed a most susceptible disposition beneath the depths.

"Oh, your ladyship!" said Cook. The others began to get more nervous. Cook's sniveling had a most depressing effect. "Cheer up," said her ladyship. "Let us look the matter squarely in the face!" That braced them a little. "Apparently my conduct has been shocking to a high sense of British respectability. Or, shall we say, morality?" "We might, your ladyship!" From Jane. "So far, so good! Now we should get on. A regular happy family!" Her ladyship beamed. "Is we 'appy?" said Pelton. "Perfectly," said her ladyship. "Your ladyship is 'appy?" With awe. "So happy!" "Account of 'im?" From Jane. "The 'uman-tiger!" From Pelton. "Well, he hasn't eaten me up, yet!" said the lady.

"What will the neighbors say?" said Pelton. "Oh! You fear for my—" "That's it!" "But he's on the other side of the house." "He's in the house, alone with your ladyship! That is, this part of the 'ouse!" "Dear me!" "Your ladyship will h'overlook our com-ing— your ladyship has always encouraged us to come to your ladyship—" "Your ladyship has always been most kind—" "And that's what makes it 'arder!"Another faint snivel from Cookie! "Yes, I believe I have always paid you high wages and given you unusual privileges," said her ladyship. "Your ladyship 'as!" "We appreciates that." "If we didn't, we should 'ave come to your lady-ship and asked for our discharges at onest," said Jane. "Dear me, I have had a narrow escape. Which brings us to the point—what are we going to do, next?" "Pack 'im off, your ladyship," said Jane.

"But if he won't go?" "Make him!" "Will you, Pelton?" "I 'umbly begs to be h'excused, your ladyship." Her ladyship made a gesture. "You see? And I fear it is his intention to prolong his visit indefinitely!" "Then I leaves," said Jane. "I 'as to!" said Pelton. "Me, too!" From James. "I has to follow suit, your ladyship," said Tommy mournfully. "Zee morality of ze country of my adop-tion compels me, likewise, to give zee notice of my departure," said Jacques. "And you, Cook?" said her ladyship. Cook's louder weeping was an affirmation. "Well," said the lady, sadly and re-signedly, "don't think I am blaming you!"

"Were it a love-potion, your ladyship?" inquired Jane. "A what?"said her ladyship. "A love-potion?" A shriek of laughter burst from her ladyship's lips. Pelton looked at Jane and Jane looked at Pelton. "Is this madness?" said their eyes. "I have it," said her ladyship suddenly. "What?" said Pelton, jumping. "The solution! I will have a chaperon." "A chaperon?" "What is simpler?" "But who?" From Pelton. "One of you!" "Us, your ladyship!" "Yes; I'll promote one of you to be chaperon!" Her eyes swept over them. "Cook!" "Me?" stammered the cook. "And you shall occupy a room of my suite! What could be more eminently respectable and satisfying to that high sense of morality? And now, of course, you will all withdraw your notices."

"And everything is lovely and pleasant, once more. And— good night! So good of you to come! No, Cook, you must not seek to escape. You are to remain. To guard my morals! What a comfortable feeling, to have some one to guard your morals! It makes one feel so free. Just like a bird! Such an absence of personal responsibility! Good night!" They trailed away and her ladyship stretched her arms. "Just like a bird," she repeated. "I waive all sense of responsibility. What a delightful feeling! Enter!" "Me?" "Chaperons, first!" said her ladyship and, with a shriek of laughter, pushed her in. "Zee morality of ze country of my adoption, eet is magnifique!" said Jacques, down in servants' hall, a little later. "Cook won't stand no nonsense from him," said Jane.

"Her can 'andle even a 'uman-tiger," said Pelton. "Her has a fist like a 'ammer!" "And think what would happen if she fell on him!" said Tommy. "In cyse he took it in 'is 'ead to walk in 'is sleep!" murmured Pelton. "My eye, she'd give 'im a head!" "Anyhow, I feels more comfortable," said Jane virtuously. "Zee morality of ze country of my adoption—"began Jacques. "Shut up!" said Tommy.

Alexander did not walk in his sleep, and the night passed uneventfully. Her ladyship and her chaperon breakfasted à la française, in their suite. Jane brought in the things. "Am I to serve 'er?" said Jane, eying the cook, reclining gorgeously, if in somewhat bewildered fashion, on a dainty settee several sizes too small for her. "Of course," said her ladyship from another settee. "As my chaperon it would be highly improper if you did not." Jane's lips tightened. "I ain't never served such as her," she remarked rebelliously. "It's the likes of her, begging your ladyship's pardon, what should be a-waitin' on me!" "I'm sure I ain't arsking anybody to wyte on me," said Cookie plaintively.

"I wanted to go down and cook my own 'am and h'eggs." "Ham and eggs!" cried her ladyship. "You have graduated from ham and eggs. You have now reached the proud dejeûner-à-la-fourchette period of life, Cook." "Bless my heart!" said Cook. That sounded like a disease. "You no longer eat. You partake of viands." "Bless my heart!" "There's a difference." Cook looked at a small egg-shell-like cup. "Do I use that?" "For your morning chocolate!" "H'it'll break in my fingers." "You will acquire proficiency." "He 'ates chocolate." "You will learn to adore it." "Is them all I 'as with it?" Eying certain dainty little rolls about big enough to crumple in your fingers and toss to the birds. "That is all. It is not ladylike to gormandize."

"But I ayn't a lydy!" "You are my chaperon." "I has been accustomed to 'earty food." "Two bloaters, ham, fried eggs, and a 'ole pot of coffee!" From Jane, viciously. "Sometimes I has a pair of kidneys for a chynge," said the cook dreamily. "Eat kidneys, reclining, à la française! Impossible!" exclaimed her ladyship. "I am sure you'd have horrid indigestion." "I could eat sitting up," suggested Cook. "And so spoil the picture? Equally impossible!"

"Is it a part of my duties that I has to wait on 'er, your ladyship?" asked Jane, coming back once more to what was troubling her. "It is!" "'Er, a-reclining there, like one of those 'orrid h'immoral French lydies, a-waiting for their lovers!" "I ayn't a-waiting for a lover!" exclaimed Cook indignantly.

"When you breakfast à la française, you must recline à la française," interposed her ladyship gently. "You have the wrong idea, Jane, quite!" "Well, 'er don't look respectable, reclinin' there like that! I ayn't criticizing your ladyship's doing it—far from me! But 'er's too big!" "Merely a charming embonpoint!" said her ladyship. "Well, if h' it breaks down, don't be blyming me!" "I won't, Jane." Sweetly. "And now, leave the things." "I ayn't saying I'll continue to wyte on 'er, your ladyship," observed Jane, bristling, once more. "'Er whose father was a butcher and 'er mother peddled fish! And not from a shop—" "Don't you be aspergili' the character of my mother!" cried Cookie, a note of belligerency in her voice. "With my own eyes has I seen 'er," went on Jane. "A horrid push-around, on wheels, and 'er, perhaps with a drop or two too much—"

"That will do," said her ladyship. And when her ladyship spoke like that her words carried conviction. Cookie sank back; she was heaving with emotion. And as she expanded and contracted thus, she looked larger than ever on the tiny settee. Jane bristled but went. When her ladyship's eyes flashed like that it meant business, and Jane had not the temerity to oppose her. But she carried her grievance below. "Cook's a-reclinin' on a settee in her ladyship's boudoir," she told Pelton. "R-reclinin' in a robe!" "Great 'eavens!" said Pelton. "W'at is h'it become? A mad'ouse!" "My eye!" said Tommy. "A-eatin' of a wafer and a thimbleful of cocoa for her breakfast!" went on Jane. Tommy began to roll up with laughter. "And her such a stuffer! I say, this is a joke!" Jane relaxed. "Maybe it is," she said. "Her ladyship called it promotion." "And her dreamin' of bloaters and collops and herrings! Ho, ho!"

"Maybe it ayn't promotion," said Jane thoughtfully. "My eye, I'd like to see her!" Jane cheered up. "There's somethink in that wye of looking at it," she conceded. What she meant was she might not find it such a task, under the circumstances, to wait on poor Cookie. It wouldn't, really, be waiting on her; it would be, secretly, gloating over her! Alexander sat up in the royal bed, stretched himself, and yawned. "Did some one knock?" "H'l, sir," said Pelton. "I thought you'd be having your bawth, sir. And 'ere's the Times, sir! And what will you be having for breakfast, sir?" "Breakfast?" Alexander seemed to wake more fully. "Breakfast; ah, you said breakfast?"

"What will you have?" "What you got?" Pelton, considering, no doubt, the best way to soothe a 'uman-tiger is to feed him, answered with an ingratiating smile: "Her ladyship 'as a most bountiful larder. Everything on 'and in season! If you has a fair appetite—" "I have!" Promptly. Get all you can while you can, no doubt, was his philosophy! Or, eat while the eating's good! "How would a small styke do?" "Rare," said Alexander. "H'underdone, of course!" from Pelton, hastily. 'Uman-tigers would, naturally, like it that way. "For a delicacy, might I suggest 'ard-boiled plover s h'eggs!" "And the plover!" suggested Alexander. "We has several, 'anging. And 'ow about a bit of lemon sole, or a cold weal-and-'ammer? Or a bite of wenison pie, from 'er lady-ship's own estates in Scotland?" "She got lands there, too?" said Alexander, betraying new interest. "A werry h'imposing estate h'it is, with fine salmon fishing!"

"Good!" said Alexander. "I'll learn to fish!" Pelton's heart sank. "'Er ladyship won't be going there for several months." "I'll wait!" "Here?" "Of course!" "Is there anythink else you'd partic-ularly fancy for breakfast?" said Felton sadly. "Cabbage soup!" "Cabbage?" "Soup," said Alexander. "For breakfast, sir?" said the horrified Pelton. "H'l—h'l don't think we 'as any cabbages h'on 'and at the moment, sir." "Couldn't you—ha!—go out and kill a few?" With a ferocious grin. "Kill?" murmured the bewildered

Pelton. "Oh, h'it's hares you are thinkin' h'of!" "Bring what you got," said Alexander bruskly. "I eat here?" "Yes, sir." "Not with her?"

"'Er ladyship breakfasts alone, with the co — I mean 'er chaperon." "Which?" "Chaperon, sir!" "Is it an animal?" said Alexander. "You mean her dog, or her cat?" Pelton again looked horrified. "H'it's a female animal of the 'uman sex," he explained. "'Er was the cook, and is now the chaperon. We 'as thought h'it more 'ighly respectable." Alexander pondered. Perhaps there was some sense in all this but it was hard to get at. "If we 'adn't thought of h'it, somebody might 'ave been pointin' his finger at 'er ladyship!" "Point his finger at her!" said Alexander. "H'accusingly!" "Point his finger at her, would he?" said Alexander fiercely. "Bah! I'd bite it off!" "But that wouldn't help," said Pelton. "H'it would only make h'it worse." "Let me catch him!" "No, no," said Pelton. "H'it wouldn't do h'at h'all! We 'as to be diplomatic. You can't bite off the finger of 'igh respectability. Begging your pardon, sir, h'it can't be done. And"—more firmly—"h'it would be 'ighly improper h'and immoral to attempt h'it."

"I'd like to try," said Alexander, with characteristic persistency. "You show me the finger!" "We 'as disposed of the finger, sir. 'Er ladyship 'erself thought of this wye!" "She bit it off?" "'Er ladyship! Ha, ha! Just your little joke, sir! 'Er ladyship hasn't a bloodthirsty 'air, sir, in 'er 'ead! 'Er bite is in 'er brain, sir!" Alexander pondered. "She has a 'ead, her ladyship 'as." Proudly. "You mean she likes to talk!" "When the gentlemen are around, sir, 'er ladyship is the center of attraction!" "Ha!" said Alexander. "Have to stop that!" "You'd be a-curtailin' of her ladyship's liberty of action?" Heavens, what a 'old!

'Of course," said Alexander, yawning. Then he frowned. "What is it?" "What?" "Chap—chap—" "Chaperon?" "Yes, that's it." "Ha! there it is! I mean, 'er!" Pointing out of the window. Alexander sat up higher in the bed and looked out upon the parklike expanse. Two figures were walking in the park; one was her ladyship; the other— "That's 'er! The chaperon! 'Er that was the cook." "It's a woman," said Alexander. "H'of course!" "A fine woman," added Alexander. "She 'as her qualities." "A big woman!" "She 'as a circumference," conceded Pelton. "I like big women," said Alexander. Pelton gazed at him with weird fascination.

"What a side view she has!" murmured Alexander. "Just the same h'all h'around, I should say!" "Just as fine, you mean!" "That might be a way of putting h'it!" "You don't agree with me?"- Fiercely. "By h'all means!" Quickly. "I'd like to see the man that says she ain't a fine woman," said Alexander. "There ayn't a finer in h'all h'England," said Pelton hastily. "That's all right," said Alexander. "Now you got some sense." "Yes, sir; thank you, sir!" "But you'd show more if you hurried up that breakfast." "Yes, sir! At once, sir!" "And never mind all those things. Bring up what you got. I'm in a hurry to get out." "You are?" stammered Pelton. "You bet," said Alexander. And glanced from the window.

"Great 'eavens!" thought Pelton. "What now? Poor Cookie! Little does she dream—" "You still here?" roared Alexander. "Going!" And Pelton fled. At the same time Alexander sprang from the bed.

Chapter XV
New Perplexities

"Oh, look who's coming!" said her lady-ship to Cookie, the chaperon. "How gorgeous!" said Cookie. "Real English!" observed her ladyship proudly. "Hasn't he 'andsome legs?" said Cookie. "Do you wonder that man makes a strange impression on me?" said her ladyship dreamily. "I'd wonder if he didn't!" said Cookie. "He fairly do make my heart go pit-a-pat!" "Eh!" said her ladyship sharply. "Remember who you are, and what! In your present position you are supposed to be coldly and unemotionally observant. You are supposed to be secretly suspicious." "Of 'im!" said Cookie. "So 'andsome!"

"That is the very reason you are suspicious!" Severely. "You are to think he harbors designs. Evil designs! You are to be my prop—my support! Without you to protect me from him, I am lost! Do you hear? Lost!" "Dear me!" In distress. "Is h' it as bad as that?" "Worse!" All this time Alexander was approaching. Alexander, in tweeds, with an English brier stuck in his mouth! Again, a new, a different, a transformed Alexander! Straight; erect; leisurely- looking; commanding! The look of a landowner in his eyes—an English landowner at that! Lord of all he surveyed and jolly well satisfied with it! Approval of the park in his eyes; of the few bits of statuary; of her ladyship, and, no doubt of it! —of Cookie! "Acts as if he thought all this goes with me!" murmured the lady, but not for Cook to hear. "Or, rather, I go with it! And, oh! how the fancied ownership of a bit of land does take the crook out of a man's spine! And his jaw, too!— I declare, it's lifted. Has a regular Hercules kind of a set, now! And, oh! what would people say if they knew who he really is, and worst of all, what he is, to me? And what shall I do about it? If I tell, it will be awful; if I don't it's just as bad."

Part of this she half-whispered; part of it she said to herself.

"What am I to do with him?" she now said in a louder voice. "Is your ladyship arsking me?" said Cookie. "I'm asking any one. I'd call it aloud from the steeples. Remember"—in a sterner tone—"suspicion, distrust, watchfulness! That's your role! Under no circumstances are you to leave me alone with him." "Morning!" said Alexander, approaching. Were his manners improving with his clothes? The word didn't fall from his lips exactly like a jolt. He didn't quite bark it out. The lady smiled sweetly. She seemed to go with the primroses and the daisies and the delicately carved marble bench.

"Good morning," she said. But Alexander was not looking at her now. His. gaze was for Cookie. "I saw you from the window," he said to Cookie. "Did you, now?" said Cookie, palpitating. Alexander eyed her steadily. "You ask Pelton! He'll tell you what I said!" Cookie moved uneasily. There was an awesome intentness in Alexander's gaze. "How werry kind! Werry kind, I'm sure!" Cookie managed to murmur. "No,"said Alexander, louder, and standing over her with glowering look, "I couldn't help it!" "Bless my 'eart!" said Cookie, beginning to wriggle. "You ask Pelton!" repeated Alexander. "Ask him to tell you what I said." Cookie began to look around uneasily. There was a light in Alexander's eye highly disconcerting.

British modesty quailed beneath it. Alexander was as brazen as the unspeakable Oriental potentate, appraising the fair charms of a pulchritudinous victim displayed in the slave-mart. Unbounded approval for too pronounced embonpoint gleamed from his shameless eyes. "A whopper!" he said. "Any one ever call you a whopper?" "H'l—h'l—"began Cookie, but could go no farther. "H'um!" said Alexander. What he implied was: "Yum! yum!" Cookie showed symptoms of almost supernatural embarrassment. Alexander bestowed upon her a most immoral wink, and Cookie got up. "Where are you going?" cried her ladyship. "Just going!" stammered Cookie. "Is this the way you fulfil the duties of your new position?" expostulated her ladyship. "I 'ands in my resignation at onct!" faltered Cookie.

"Nonsense!" said her ladyship sharply. "I'd follow," said Alexander. Cookie did not answer; she could not; but she did the next best thing. She fled. "Wait!" said Alexander. She fled faster. "A nice way for a chaperon to act!" called out her ladyship. Even this did not stop her. She continued to flee like a fawn. "You ask Pelton!" shouted Alexander after her. Cookie disappeared. "Exit chaperon!" sighed the lady. "Now, what am I to do?" Alexander continued to stand motionless, gazing in the direction the vanished fair one had gone. He seemed meditating. "As a disorganizer of households," said her ladyship, regarding him with justifiable displeasure, "I would match you against all comers!" Alexander did not answer.

"I suppose," observed the lady, "it's the near proximity of your country to the Oriental countries that makes you so! Temperamental contiguity! you might call it. Like smallpox, or the measles! No accounting for taste! But I am disappointed! You looked so nice and English and phlegmatic!—last night, I mean. And your conduct has been so perfect and highly respectable— with me, I mean! A modem knight! Ha! And now?" She sighed. "Isn't it awful? Oh, Alexander!" Still Alexander did not answer. Was the man made of stone? "He does not hear me," said the lady. Alexander folded his arms and puffed at his pipe. His gaze was fixed on vacancy. At that moment Pelton approached excitedly. "'Er's gone! The cook!" he cried. "'Er left in a hurry, and arsked to have 'er things sent h'after 'er!" "Did she ask you what he "—indicating Alexander—"said?"

"She did, and that seemed to finish her! She's a-walkin' down the lane for dear life at this blessed minute. Fleein' from 'im! The 'uman- tiger!" "It isn't his fault, Pelton," said the lady in sweet sad tones. "It's his being born in a country contiguous!" "What's that, your ladyship?" "Contiguous! That's what caused it." "What, your ladyship?" stammered Pelton. "Like measles, or smallpox, Pelton!" "Bless my heart! 'As 'e them?" "A figure of speech—

that is all!" "Is h'it?"Dubiously. "Which brings us to:What next?" Her ladyship spoke almost wearily. Her attitude was that of one trying to bear up—to be brave against frightful odds, perhaps. "That is the question," Pelton groaned. "We mustn't forget that high morality we are guardians of, Pelton!" Impressively. Pelton looked more miserable. The lady bore up better and better. Blood will count. "I have it," she said suddenly.

"Have you?" said Pelton more hopefully. "Yes, yes!" She waved her little hand. "I'll —I'll have a dog!—a big dog, for a chaperon! A savage dog! He'll lie at my feet by day and sleep at my door by night." It was plain that Pelton, in spite of his respect for the lady, and her reputation for cleverness, did not think much of this suggestion. "'E'd be making friends with 'im!" Jerking his thumb toward the motionless Alexander. "A-feeding him 'igh and making friends with 'im!" "I suppose so!" Resignedly. "He'd have 'im a-licking his 'and, your ladyship, and wagging his tail, instead of tyking chunks out of 'is legs!" "'Is 'andsome legs!" murmured her ladyship absently. "H'l beg your ladyship's pardon!" Horrified. "Oh, the remark is not original!" Hastily. "It's only a quotation, Pelton."

"H'oh!" Dubiously. Of course, that wasn't quite the same as if the remark had been original with her ladyship. "Which being the case, it would be a pity, all the same, now, wouldn't it?" "W'ot?" "To have chunks taken out of them?" Pelton's chest rose and fell. "I'd like—" "Wait!" said her ladyship. Pelton waited. Her manner was impressive. "I have it!—This time!—Really!" "W'ot?" Bewildered. "The chaperon! The new one! And how to keep her! Yes, yes; I've got it!" Vivaciously. "How to circumvent him. For embonpoint we'll substitute—attenuation!" "W'ot's that, your ladyship?" "I'll have a chaperon thin as a pop-hole!" Pelton brightened. "A 'uman lath!" he murmured, "with a fyce like a 'atchet!" Pelton positively smiled. The 'uman-tiger wouldn't be licking his chops over 'er!

"There's Liza Jane Handsaw, down in the village," said her ladyship. "With a fyce like a 'and-saw!"chuckled Pelton. "I'm sure she'd be glad to come!" "Tickle her to death," said Pelton. "She 'ates real work. She'd tyke to reclining. And when I think of her fyce, and w'ot the 'uman-tiger will think when 'e sees her, if it weren't for your ladyship's presence, h'l just 'ave to laugh!" "Is this a laughing matter?" Reproachfully. "No, no! Go at once and fetch her!" "At once, your ladyship!" Pelton started to go. At the same time, Alexander turned to walk away. "Where can 'im be going, your ladyship?" ventured Pelton. "Not after her!" "Liza?" "The other!—the cook," said her ladyship. "If he do, he won't find 'er!" said Pelton. "Her'll be 'ome and 'iding before this, your ladyship! He was going like a double-six, twelve- horse-power hen, down the 'ighway, w'en larst I seen her! I won't never get near her, h'any more!" "I trust not," breathed her ladyship. There was a faraway look in her eyes. "I tremble to think—but I must not think! Go, go!" Imperiously. "And do not fail me, Pelton! If you failed me?" "No?" said Pelton. "Handsaw, with a face like a hatchet!" Pelton went.

Her ladyship leaned back on the marble-bench in the garden. In the bushes at her elbow the birds sang sweetly. "I wonder," she said to herself, gazing in the direction Alexander had gone, "was it Cook, or —a public-house that has drawn him from my side?" Then an enigmatic smile swept her lips. "The latter, no doubt," she sighed. Which was not far from wrong! Alexander, not long thereafter, did turn into a public tavern—and not into the compartment reserved for the common herd, if you please! No; Alexander strode into the pew reserved for the gentry. And such was his bearing that he deceived even the barmaid. Now, when a man can deceive a barmaid, he is some deceiver.

Chapter XVI
An Echo from the Past

"I haven't seen her before," said Alexander, staring at Miss Eliza Jane Handsaw. "No," said her ladyship. "She's just come. She's to take Cook's place." "She!" said Alexander incredulously. "Take her place! Haw! haw!" "I didn't come here to be insulted," said Miss Handsaw, rising stiffly. "It's only his way," said her ladyship quickly. Heavens! was she going to lose her new chaperon almost before she had entered upon her duties? "His playful ways with the ladies!" "Oh," said Miss Handsaw, "if he only means to be plyful I like a bit of plye myself, on occasions!" "Yes, play is good for us all," said her ladyship soothingly.

"And Alexander is like a big Newfoundland dog, always tumbling over somebody's finer susceptibilities! But he doesn't mean anything, and we that know him well do not mind." "If it's only plye, I don't mind," said Miss Handsaw. "I has a special passion for Newfoundland dogs and kittens and all animals, whether of the higher or the lower order, that likes to plye!" The look she cast upon Alexander was both forgiving and beaming. It seemed to convey the alarming intelligence: "If you want to plye, come on!" "I used especially to adore 'ide-and-seek when I was a few years younger," she added. "It's such fun to 'ide!" Looking at Alexander. "I'd like to," said Alexander sullenly. He seemed to regard it as a mean trick on her ladyship's part—this substitution of a "bean-pole" for a "whopper!" Miss Handsaw stiffened.

"Ha, ha!" said her ladyship blithely. "More of his playful ways!" "Is it plyeful?" asked Miss Handsaw suspiciously. "Couldn't be anything else!" said her ladyship. "That last sounded like an aspersion," said Miss Handsaw. "Alexander is quite incapable of a double-entendre. If he says he likes to hide, it is that he still retains that happy predilection of young boyhood. Isn't it, Alexander?" "Humph!" said Alexander, obviously disgruntled! "Is that plyeful?" asked Miss Handsaw. "Of course! The trouble is, Alexander hasn't yet had his lunch. He's waiting! He's hungry! All men are like that when they're hungry! He's thinking of cold cuts of rare beef; of moldy old cheese; and greens, yes, greens! Ah, we mustn't forget the greens. Now look at him. See him brighten! See him change at the prospect of greens!"

And truly, Alexander did look less disgruntled. How could a mere man listen to her ladyship's enumeration without brightening? Especially after that long walk he had taken after leaving the village inn! "You see, Miss Handsaw's going to be our chaperon," went on her ladyship brightly. "Got to have her around all the time?"said Alexander. "Ha! ha!" laughed her ladyship. "What a way he has! Isn't he funny?" "Ha! ha!" said Miss Handsaw dubiously. Alexander's sense of humor and playful ways got a bit on her nerves. But her ladyship's wages were high, and the thought of them helped Miss Handsaw preserve her poise. "Yes," said her ladyship, "we may expect to have the pleasure of Miss Handsaw's presence for an indefinite period. Where we are, she will be!" "For why?" said Alexander.

"English respectability," said the lady. "It's far from my desire to intrude," said Miss Handsaw stiffly. "Intrude? Oh, dear! We are delighted," said her ladyship quickly. If she lost Miss Handsaw what should she do? "As I was saying to Alexander, where can we find another such as Miss Handsaw for our purpose? And what did he say? What did you say, Alexander?" "I"— began Alexander. "Was it not:'Where, indeed'?"— "It was"— began Alexander. "Not!" he was about to add, but her ladyship went on:"It's very hard to understand Alexander. He likes to show people the other side of himself." "The plyeful side!" said Miss Handsaw, relaxing. "I"—once more began Alexander.

"Let us eat!" said her ladyship quickly. "It is time. More than time! What a waste of time!" she rattled on, to cover up Alexander's delinquencies. "Rare roast beef; Scotch mutton; jugged hare!"—she thought the last would surely engross Alexander's attention, and it did. Alexander forgot what he had been about to say. Also, he appeared less resentful, once more, of Miss Handsaw's presence. Why bother about Handsaws when hares assailed your mental vision? What mattered if she had a face like a hatchet, or a form like a bean-pole? Alexander started impetuously toward the dining-room. "Kindly give your arm to Miss Handsaw," said her ladyship. And Alexander obeyed. Possibly he told himself that a quick compliance was the shortest route to jugged hare. Miss Handsaw might be a bean-stalk, but if at the top of the bean-stalk hung a hare?—Alexander, under the circumstances, could not do less than escort the beanstalk to the hare. "Isn't he a regular Chesterfield?" said her ladyship proudly. "Which reminds me, he, too, was very fond of jugged hare!"

"What a coincidence!" said Miss Handsaw. "Yes," said her ladyship, with a happy smile. "Alexander reminds me of him in more ways than one."

"And now," said her ladyship, as they smoked their after-lunch cigarettes in the library, "would you mind, my dear Miss Handsaw, if I had a word in private with Alexander? I believe a chaperon may extend that latitude to her charge. What is your opinion? Would it be proper?" "'Ighly," said Miss Handsaw, who on occasions sawed off an "H." "And I always likes to be obliging." "Thank you so much! Of course you are not to leave the room." "How would it be if I strolled out upon the balcony?" "Good!" said Alexander. "Not at all," said her ladyship, so quickly as not to give Miss Handsaw time to think. "You see, far be it from me to stretch a point where the proprieties are concerned. If, now, you were to retire to the other side of the room?"

"Delighted!" said Miss Handsaw. Sympathy for lovers' sweet confidences in her eyes! "You see, I have something very important to say to Alexander!" "Naturally," said Miss Handsaw with perfect understanding and tact. "Something that would not do for other ears!" "Naturally," said Miss Handsaw once more. As she spoke, she smiled on Alexander. Alexander shuddered. Miss

Handsaw sighed. Love's young dream was so sweet! "Why does she look at me like that?" said Alexander. "Fie!" said her ladyship timidly. Miss Handsaw moved with little mincing steps across the room. She tried not to make her going too apparent—but just as if she were fading away through her own volition, and not because she had been requested to do so. Nothing could have been more delicate! "What a charming girl!" breathed her ladyship, as Miss Handsaw deftly coiled herself upon a great couch on the far side of the room. "Girl!" said Alexander. "I think we shall get on very nicely." "Shall we?" said Alexander ominously. "I don't like 'em that way." "What way?" "Up and down! I like 'em when they grow sidewise." "We can remedy that very nicely," said her ladyship blithely. Alexander regarded her suspiciously. "I'll get you one of those magic-mirrors that make people look fat—the kind they have in museums!—and I'll arrange it so you shall always see Miss Handsaw reflected!" "Rot!" said Alexander. The lady made a gesture; then her face became serious.

"How can we jest at such a moment! Alexander, I have some very serious news to impart. I have just received a note from the Honorable Bertie Brindleton." "Who's he?" "A man! A man I was half-engaged to before I met you!" "Half-engaged?" "There was, I believe, a partial understanding. At least, I think there was. You see, our two estates are contiguous." "You mean you meant to marry him?" "Half-meant," confessed the lady. "Ha, ha!" said Alexmider. "Why this brutal levity?" "He gets left!" The lady drew herself up. "I beg your pardon," she said. "It is, really, very awkward. To explain, I mean! You see, I haven't yet told any one our secret—our dreadful secret! Necessarily, it will have to come out." "I don't mind."

"No; I imagine not. But it will be hard to tell Bertie." "Let me tell him!" "He will be terribly put out!" "Smash him, if he doesn't like it!" boasted Alexander. "You!—Smash an Honorable—the son of an earl!" "I smash him just the same if he's a son-of-a-gun!" bragged Alexander. "You don't understand. This matter is too delicate to be remedied by the smashing process. And the question is; Would Bertie marry a divorcee?" "A which?" "Me? After I have unmarried you?" "Un?" repeated Alexander. "You think, then, I give you up?" "You won't?" Gazing at him weirdly fascinated. "I like it blame well here!" "But, don't you see, you are only an incident?"

"An hymeneal June-bug! You flutter a brief connubial moment, and then, your gay marital adventure comes to an end." "June-bug, eh?" said Alexander, tapping his expansive chest. "You mean an eagle! That's more the kind of a bird I am! What I grab in my claws I keep!" "An eagle?" said the lady, shrinking before Alexander's predatory gaze. "Honorable Bertie!"scoffed Alexander. "When I hit him, his head crack like an egg-shell. Feel my muscle!" The lady laid a shy little hand on his arm. She was much impressed. "What an awful bulge!" she exclaimed. And truly, Alexander had the biceps of an Atlas, while his shoulders, to her startled eyes, seemed almost big enough to bear the world. In his new clothes, he had, oddly enough, acquired a new physical grace. When he navigated about the drawing room his movements made her think of a big tiger. At such moments, Alexander was eminently satisfying.

One might, under happier circumstances, feel cozily comfortable in his proximity. "A June-bug, eh?" he jibed once more. "He put me out? Ho, ho!" "But our agreement?" said the lady sadly. "Was it not the understanding, you were to permit me to unmarry you? Did you not so agree?" "I change my mind!" Brazenly. "Any man can do that! Tell me, you never change your mind?" The lady did not answer. What could she say? Alexander's line of argument was quite overpowering. "You change your mind sometimes; I change my mind; all people change their mind! What you say to that?" "I'm afraid it is useless to argue the point." "Isn't this good enough?" said Alexander, looking around him. "Nice place to sleep; good clothes; plenty beer; plenty meat!" "Such appreciation!" mused the lady. "Right from the heart, too, unless I am mistaken. These sentiments are genuine." "You bet!" said Alexander. "Can one eliminate a guest, so appreciative?" Alexander grinned. "Not easy! Maybe I never go!" "Never! But this is too much!—too flattering!" "You see!" Confidently. "Words!—idle words! You but say that, thinking to—to please me! Soon you would grow bored; tire of it all; of me—" "I don't mind you!" "But you might! You would." "No," he said. "I like to hear you talk." The lady caught her breath. "Did you say, 'like'?" "Sure!" Imperturbably. "But since when?" "I get used to it." "But why do you like it?" "I think of a lot of birds making a fuss in the bushes," said Alexander.

The lady gazed at him in amazement. Here was a side to Alexander totally unexpected. A different Alexander from the one who had glowered upon Cookie! "'A lot of birds fussing,' "she repeated. "Yes," said Alexander non-amorously. In fact, he had seemed rather bored at the turn the conversation had taken. "And do you—approve of birds?" "I don't mind them." "But, wouldn't you get to mind them?" Alexander pondered. "No." "But why do you not disapprove of birds?" persisted the lady. "They make a nice sound." "This is a revelation!"Not of the birds—but of Alexander! "Once I kept a bird, in a cage," he remarked. "You?" "Sure! It sang me awake." "Sang you awake?" "In the morning!"

"You—you mean, it saved you the expense of an alarm-clock?" "That's so," said Alexander practically. "Only it stopped singing, and then I let it go." "Why?" "Too much money to feed it!" "Oh!" "Besides, what's the use of a bird that doesn't sing you awake?" "How eminently practical! And then you got an alarm-clock instead?" "No!" "Cost too much?" "No! Alarm-clock sings you awake too quick! Gives you the hippety-hops! B-r-r-r-r!" Alexander shivered. "Oh?" Somewhere, in the depths of Alexander's profundities, lay a delicate supersensitiveness. "Perhaps you are right!" Languidly. "I dare say you are! But"—suddenly—"what has all this got to do with the Honorable Bertie, and the predicament you have get me into? And what in the world shall I say to him when he comes here?" "He is coming here?" Slowly. "To-day!" "To-day?" "Yes, and oh!"—looking out of the window— "there he is!" "Ha!" said Alexander, with a tigerish smile. "Go, go!" implored the lady. "Let me break the news to him gradually. Let me prepare him by slow degrees for the awful truth." "I like to see him," said Alexander grimly. "I like to see this Honorable Bertie!" "But not now, I beg! Do not make it harder. Go, I implore! Dear, dear Alexander!" Alexander hesitated. "All right! But if he make a fuss, you call me." "Yes, yes; I promise!" Alexander started to go; then he turned. "You think he kill you?" he asked with mild curiosity. "Englishmen do not go to that extremity." "In my country we use knife! Maybe I better stay, with long roast-beef carving knife under my coat?" "No, no! Your solicitude is deeply touching, and, believe me, I am truly grateful, but—" "You like me?" said Alexander. What was that—a spark in his eye? "Like?" said the lady.

"You not like, I not go!" "But you must—don't you see?" "Then say you like me!" "I—I—oh, dear! He's almost at the door. They must not meet like this! Go, go!" Alexander folded his arms. "You got to say." "Oh, well—I like—like—anything you like! I —I adore you, Alexander! You—you are all that is wonderful—magnificent! You—you are the apple of my eye! The— the—is that enough? I trust that will do?" Alexander grinned triumphantly. "Ho, ho!" he said. "Yes, that will do. You tell him that! I got good joke on Honorable Bertie."

"You—you call it a joke?" "Make him feel good! Ha, ha!"And Alexander went. "What a fearful man!" said her ladyship, gazing after him. "And what have I said? But I had to! To save Bertie's life! Wouldn't you have done it?" Feverishly, crossing to Miss Handsaw. "What?"said Miss Handsaw, unwinding herself. "Tell a fib to save a human life!" "That would depend on whose!" said Miss Handsaw.

CHAPTER XVII
CROSS-PURPOSES

The Honorable Bertie entered the room. He paused at sight of the lady. "I say, how jolly!" "Jolly!" "Isn't it, though?" But there was a trace of constraint in Bertie's tones. "Is it?" "You are looking fit!" "You, too!" "Thanks, awfully!" Bertie came forward awkwardly. There was a slightly guilty look in his eye which her ladyship, usually so observant, did not, at the present moment, notice. "I say, this is jolly!" repeated the Honorable Bertie, taking her hand. He was big and blond. Alexander was big and dark. Both were fine looking men—quite opposite! Both were husky, too, and strong.

Her ladyship wondered which was stronger? Alexander, no doubt! She felt a wild desire to ask Bertie to let her feel his arm. "This is jolly," said the Honorable Bertie once more. The lady shivered. "I wish you wouldn't repeat yourself, Bertie!" "Repeat?" "You see, I particularly detest that word, 'jolly,' and I'm going to ask you a frank question, Bertie." Nothing like taking the bull, or Bertie, by the horns! "When we last parted, did you consider we were—what shall I call it?—partially engaged?" The Honorable Bertie looked embarrassed. He had taken the lady's hand doubtfully. Even when he had said: "Awfully jolly!" There had been a furtive expression in his usually open gaze. "I—" He now stammered. "Well, to tell you the truth, there might have been a—a partial—"

"Would you go as far as to say we were half- engaged?" interrupted the lady anxiously. "Or, would you even reduce the fraction further? Say, an eighth-engaged?" Bertie looked at the lady quickly. Sometimes his slow brain was overtaken by fugitive glimmerings. "An eighth-engaged?" he muttered, eyes still on the lady. "That is rather a small fraction." "But"—nervously—"wasn't it, after all, only a very partial understanding? A very small frac-

81

tion of an understanding?" Bertie studied her. "I don't know as I'd go as far as that—quite!" She straightened. "The point is, how far does a very small fraction of an understanding—possibly no understanding at all!—bind one?" "Ha!" said Bertie. Just like Alexander! How like men were, in some things! "The question is:Is the fraction of a thing, the thing itself? Being so much less than the thing!"

"Ha!" said Bertie once more. "Or if," with logic irrefutable, "being only one-eighth bound, and seven-eighths not bound, or seven times not bound, to one time bound, you are not, by mere preponderance, bound at all?" Bertie stared. "What is this? A lesson in fractions? I always was weak in mathematics." "To descend to plain English, then, Bertie, I believe I—I flirted with you, just a little bit, and you, in equally plain English, responded—very slightly!" Bertie looked uncomfortable. "Any one would flirt with you!" "Thank you!" "Confound it, you know it!" "Thank you, again!" "I—I never flattered myself I was the one and only man you'd flirted with, Estelle." "Is that a reproach?" Studying him. "That depends!" "On what?" "How—how far you may have gone with someone else! I know—know how many of the chaps were—were mad over you!" "Is this—jealousy?" "You might—" "Or would-be tyranny! You have no right—" "What about that fraction?" said Bertie shrewdly. "Did I altogether concede its existence?" "Didn't you?" She looked at him. "If one flirts a little—" "I should say it depends on how far—" Was he trying to trap her? "I don't concede it went far at all, with you!" A little breathlessly. Bertie bowed like a gentleman. "That's for you to say!" The lady blushed. Then she drew herself up proudly.. "Let's look facts in the face! It was moonlight; you did look big and handsome." Bertie looked foolish; and again that expression of vague uneasiness overspread his face. "There's something about big men that has always appealed to me!" Dreamily. "No, no! I don't mean that. How perfectly brazen and shocking!"

"Never mind!" Bertie looked uncomfortable. "I, too, forgot myself," he muttered awkwardly. "But by jove, there was some excuse; you did look—ripping!" "Nevertheless——" "Pooh! What's—what's one little one?" The lady went oh: "No words were spoken. No promises exchanged." Did her accents betoken thankfulness? Bertie's look became more searching. "Are words necessary," he said suddenly, "when heart speaks to heart?" "Oh!" gasped the lady. He took a step toward her. "Oh!" she repeated. "To what does this tend?" he said sternly. "When you speak to me like that," she said, recovering, "I deny the existence of any understanding."

"Oh, you do!" "I do! And I beg to remind you I have heard about a few of your own little affairs!" Bertie shifted abruptly. His expostulations rang, in the least, hollowly. "Here am I, hurrying up to see you, at the first opportunity, and this is the way I am received! Is it what I expected? Is it, I ask?" The lady looked unimpressed. "Shall I tell you what my feelings were, as I hurried here? The impatience?"—He suddenly checked himself. Was anything wrong with Bertie? "Are you sure you didn't forget me?" Clear eyed, she regarded him. "Forget?" He threw out a hand. "Could I?" Half-bitterly. "That kiss!" His tones were hoarse. "Could any man forget—" "Perhaps not," said the lady calmly, "if it had been a real one! If my heart had gone with it! But as it was—a mere peck! And—it seemed one way to stop your foolish conduct. Indeed I quite absolve myself of the incident!"

"You do?" "I do! A peck, cold as moonlight!" "She calls it a 'peck,'" muttered Bertie. "What a word!" "And you come here, on the strength of that, hoping to force me to marry you!" Bertie looked startled. "Of—of course!" "You considered I had given my soul to you with a peck!" she demanded. "Don't call it that! I hate that word!" "You—you care for me, so much, then?" Bertie looked down. "Can you ask?" In a low depressed tone. "Or was it you felt in honor bound to come up here and ask me to marry you?" Bertie lifted a startled glance. "I —of course —well, you know—" "Quite intelligible! And intelligent!" Each studied the other now. "What has she been up to?" thought Bertie. "What has he been up to?" thought the lady. "Something awful!" thought Bertie.

"Something awful!" thought the lady. "Won't you sit down?"said the latter politely. Bertie did. "Wager she's engaged herself to some man!" he thought. "He's got over his head with Polly or Dolly, or some circus creature!" thought the lady. "Light a cigarette,"she said aloud. "Thanks!" Gloomily. The lady looked down. Was this the time to tell her awful secret? By any possibility, did Bertie care for her? His face was as long as a yardstick. And they had been chums for years! And their estates were contiguous! And had it been only and absolutely a mere "peck"? Had she cared, a very little bit? Not in the way that leads to the altar! Of that she was certain. But Bertie? Had she injured hint in her thoughts? A man might fall under the spell of a Dolly or a Polly, and still cherish a deeper, more abiding passion. And Bertie was handsome! Almost as handsome as Alexander! And Bertie was a gentleman, while Alexander was merely good to look at, with the mental equipment of a clown.

It was all very confusing. "I wonder if I have acted right?" now thought the lady. "Maybe she is free, and only sounding me," thought Bertie. "What if she has an idea I really should marry her!" Bertie wiped his brow. "Feel better?" said the lady. "Yes—no," said Bertie. The lady decided not to tell all of her secret, just then. Of course she would have to account for Alexander's and Miss Handsaw's presence in the house. And if she didn't tell all the truth, how much should she tell? She was relieved that Miss Handsaw had withdrawn to the balcony at Bertie's entrance. "How did you hear of my home-coming?" she now asked. "Lord high chancellor, told you were you overjoyed?"

"Your uncle, the lord high chancellor, told me."

"Yes, I wrote him. And you were overjoyed?"

"Of—of course!"

"I must tell him," thought the lady. "Don't say you are engaged to some other fellow!" said Bertie, as reading that impulse. "I may truthfully say, I am not engaged!" Bertie slid deeper into his chair. "Would you—have been very jealous?" said the lady. "Would I?" Loudly. "Would I?" "And if brought face to face with this hypothetical individual?" "But you are not engaged?" "No; but if I were?" "What's the object of supposing?" "Might be, then," suggested the lady. "I don't think," said Bertie slowly, "I'd like to trust myself in his presence! That is a first!" The lady laughed nervously. Then she bent over him with a sprightly look. "Bertie, would you mind—would you take it as a liberty, if I asked you to let me feel your muscle?" "Charmed!" said Bertie, and bent his forearm.

The lady's delicate fingers pursued their investigation. "Not so bad!" said Bertie with assumed indifference. He knew, indeed, his biceps were something to be proud of. "All there, eh?" But the lady only smiled enigmatically. "Poor Bertie!" she said. "What's that?" "Nothing! A mere expression of sympathy! That is all." Bertie stared. "See here, Estelle, what's all this mean?" "I wish I knew!" "Got a notion to hang around and find out!" "Did you bring your luggage?" "No." "Then how could you hang around?" "When my own place was let, last time, I came down here; I remember leaving a lot of things for Pelton to look after!" "Yes; I remember that as one of your failings."

"Easier to leave old duds at week-ends than to bother taking them away!" "Oh, there's a method in it," said Bertie. "I have lots of clothes scattered around different places where I'm expected about every so often! Under the circumstances, feeling kind of uneasy about you, I could manage to stay and get Pelton to resurrect some of my old duds." "Oh, no, you couldn't!" Wild laughter rang from her ladyship's lips. "Why not?" The lady looked out of the window. In the distance stalked Alexander imposingly arrayed in tweeds. "Ha, ha!" said her ladyship. "Why not?" said Bertie more sulkily. "Because, at present, your wardrobe is otherwise engaged." Bertie frowned. "Engaged?" "Rented out, as it were!" "But I say, Pelton has a nerve!" "It wasn't Pelton. It was I!"

"You! But confound it—" "Don't say 'confound it,' Bertie. Say what you think!" "What do you mean?" "Damn!"

Chapter XVIII
An Ominous Meeting

"And now, shall we walk in the garden?" But you haven't told me why?" "Hasn't there been enough explaining, for the present? Let us stroll and forget ourselves. I am sorry I can't provide a little moonlight—" "Eh?" "You won't take it from me as inhospitable that I don't?" "Not at all! Ha, ha!" But Bertie's laughter sounded artificial. "You're sure you're not engaged, or half-engaged, to some other fellow?" "I am not even half-engaged, Bertie. I give my sacred word of honor. I swear it on the honor of a daughter of a belted earl!" "Confound it, Estelle, I can't make you out!" he growled.

"Why try?" Merrily. "Why not take me as I am!" Bertie looked positively startled; then recovered himself. "You've been away quite a time," he said, "and I've half a mind you've had some experiences or adventures—" "Experiences!" she laughed. "I could a tale unfold—" "Unfold it, then!" "Here? How unromantic! Let us go into the garden! That identical spot!" For the moment Bertie looked scared. "Come," she said, with gay abandon. And Bertie went. As they approached a marble bench the lady spied Alexander there. At sight of them he got up. The lady stopped. "It is already occupied," she said wistfully. Bertie stared at Alexander. "My tweeds!" "You recognize them? They are rather pronounced!" Bertie did not make an amiable response. He eyed Alexander with disfavor. Alexander smiled.

"My clothes!" repeated Bertie. "Aren't they a perfect fit!" said the lady enthusiastically. "Confounded liberty, I call it!" "You should see him in your evening suit," said the lady. "I should, should I?" said Bertie, glaring at Alexander. "Only they are a bit tight across the shoulders!" "He should have them let out," said Bertie in a funny tone. "So he could. They would be a bit more comfortable." "I hope so." "He has such nice broad shoulders, it's a shame to pinch them in!" "Beastly!" said Bertie. "It's too bad your shoulders weren't a little broader," murmured the lady. And Bertie, who was rather proud of his tolerably broad shoulders, said something under his breath.

"I wouldn't," said the lady. "He's frightfully strong." Bertie again glared at Alexander. The latter smiled sweetly. He didn't offer to approach them. "No; you mustn't go any nearer," said the lady quickly to Bertie. "Don't let his sweet expression deceive you. He is really dangerous when aroused. The 'uman-tiger, Pelton calls him!" Bertie's disgust was unutterable. "Under the circumstances I might be justified in punching—" "No, no," said the lady quickly, placing a detaining hand on his arm. "Why court destruction?" "For me, or for him?" Ominously. "You, of course!" Bertie made a sound. "In that case," he said witheringly, "I had better fly." "Or flee!" Bertie turned on his heel. "Discretion is the better part of valor!" he murmured. "Indeed it is," said the lady, and they walked away.

"I hope he isn't coming after me," observed Bertie, in those same withering accents. "No, he isn't!" "I'm so frightened I daren't look around," said the Honorable Bertie, with a slight sneer. "And now, may I ask, how much rent are you getting for my clothes?" "I?" "Or, is it Pelton?" The lady giggled. "How deliciously impertinent! You are improving. Who has been improving you? Has some one been improving you?" Bertie walked a little faster. "If I did not have every faith in you, I should say some one had been sharpening your wits!" "Why can't you be serious? I come down here and find some one wearing my clothes. What am I to think? What would any man think?" "Shall I tell you the truth?" "If you"—Bertie paused—"will be so good!" he added. "Why have you rented out my clothes?"

'Oh, that was just a figure of speech. They aren't really rented." "Presented?" "I believe he considers them his." Bertie glanced over his shoulder and stopped. "Don't obey that impulse!" "Hang it, he's smoking my pipe, I believe!" burst from Bertie. "If you will leave things around! I always told you it was a bad habit!" "Anything else of mine he's preempted?" "I believe you left some shirts." "Is he wearing my shirts?" More explosively. "I say, this" "They're a little tight at the neck, and—" "I wish they'd choke him!" "You aren't jealous, are you, Bertie?" "Jealous?" Bertie's anger seemed to fade magically. "You see, he's only a castaway. We took him in. He was cast up by the sea. His garments were torn almost to tatters. He was a sight! So we fed, clothed and revivified him. Would you have had me do less? Tell him to go on—to expire in the byways, perhaps?" "You say he was shipwrecked? The fellow's only a poor sailor, or something of the kind, then?" "Something of the kind! A porter, I believe!" "He looks jolly well at home, for a—" "The tendencies of the time! Poor fellow! Why begrudge him?" Bertie didn't. A shipwrecked sailor!—His presence there seemed natural enough, and there was no reason why he shouldn't sit on a bench during the period of his convalescence. Bertie did not think, then, to inquire why Pelton had dubbed the visitor a 'uman-tiger, or to endeavor to reconcile the incongruity of bedecking the shipwrecked one in his (Bertie's) evening clothes. In his confused mental state Bertie overlooked a few questions he ordinarily would have asked. "Where are we walking?" said Bertie.

She lifted her eyes, and then Bertie blushed. The pathway before them had long been known as "Lovers' Lane." Bertie bit his lips. The lady walked on dreamily; Bertie eyed her uneasily. She was very beautiful—too beautiful! "Of course, I was only jesting about its being a partial understanding," she said. "You did think I was jesting, didn't you?" "Ye— es!" "You don't think I would let some one say— do what—you know, and then—You don't think that poorly of me!" "I—I—" Bertie didn't know what he thought. "You didn't?" In an excess of emotion. "No—oo!" Was that a sigh of relief? "I had to hear you say it. And now I do feel sure of you!" "Do-you?" "And of myself! Need I say more?" "I think not," said Bertie hoarsely. Had he not been told by Some One, only recently, no woman could resist him?

"Uncle will be so pleased!" "The lord high chancellor?" "Yes. He has frequently pointed out that the two estates are contiguous." Bertie was silent. "I am so glad you came down!" "Are you?" In a whisper. "Very!"Feverishly. "I was so afraid you wouldn't!" "Were you?" "You were as anxious to see me as I was you?" "Yes, yes! Of course!" "And you do forgive me, teasing you? About being only half -engaged?" "I half -thought you were in earnest,"-said Bertie hoarsely. "You did? Oh, Bertie! After all these years we've known each other!" "Seemed too—too good to be true!"-mumbled Bertie. "Silly boy!" Tone positively caressing! They walked on.

"Haven't you forgotten something?" Shyly. Oh, shameless! An upward look from the blue eyes flared like a spark into Bertie's remorseful and smoldering gaze. "You didn't used to be so—" The red lips curled. Brazen red lips! Mechanically, Bertie slipped an arm about that perfect waist. The lady's head inclined; so a fair flower might bend to the wooing breath of a warm summer breeze! Bertie looked down. "Home again!" sighed the lady. "Must seem fine!" muttered Bertie. "Can you ask?" Bertie stooped for a "peck." He felt obliged to. The exigencies of the situation demanded such enterprising action on his part. But to his relief she drew back. "Not now! Let us wait!" Hastily. "The moonlight! Same place!" "All right!" As if a little postponement mattered much! Nothing mattered much. "Shall we keep it a secret for a little while?" suggested the lady. "Our engagement?"

"Yes! I think we'd better," "Only for a little while!" "Make it long's you like!" "But?" "What do I care, long's we know?" Recklessly. The lady laughed joyously. She was certain now. If Bertie wasn't engaged to Polly or Dolly, or Flossie or Fluffy, why that guilty manner? Of course any one of those artful stage-hussies could get Bertie, simply by flattering him and telling him how handsome he was! Bertie had come with the intention of trapping,studying her (Estelle); he wasn't exactly sure what might be expected of him. Her ladyship determined to make Bertie pay; she would give him a bad half-hour or so. She gazed up at Bertie, more languishingly. Having reached the end of Lovers' Lane, they turned and came back again. And emerging, in lover-like fashion, whom should they encounter but Alexander!

CHAPTER XIX
A CHANCE TO RETALIATE

Her ladyship gave a gasp, knowing Alexander's truculent disposition. Too late, she realized her own awkward situation. She, a newly-wedded bride, and caught like that! A hysterical desire to laugh mingled with a vague apprehension. Would Alexander start in to annihilate Bertie, or to slay her? Hastily she disengaged herself from Bertie's arm and Bertie did not seek to detain her. Her ladyship drew herself up, expectantly. To her surprise, Alexander did not go into a mad rage and tear everything to pieces; on the contrary, the lady saw a look on his face she had never seen there before! His eyes rested on her steadily. Heavens! what a deep look! It positively seemed to pierce her.

Then Alexander drew a long breath, puffed at his pipe, and— did the last thing on earth she expected of him! He walked by. The lady stared after him. Oh, man of wonderful surprises! It was certainly interesting, having him around. Thrills emanated from his presence, or permeated his immediate proximity. Even now, gazing after his powerful receding figure, she was aware her breath came and went quickly. It was a new and novel experience, to expect to be crushed to the earth or to be ground beneath a crunching heel, and then to have absolutely nothing happen. Where Alexander was there was not monotony. For who might say the danger was over? Was it not merely deferred? The mere fact that he could control his violent temper augured ill for the future. He would plan, probably, how best to obliterate them, singly. He might even desire to show himself an artist in the gentle art of obliterating people. Would he do it with a butcher-knife or an ax? Or would he stalk them like the stealthy thug, turning the poetic Lovers' Lane into an uncanny and shivery Thugs' Ambuscade? And the lovely private lake—would that become the dark and gruesome pool for the disposal of the victims?

Poor Bertie! Into what a fate had she drawn him!

And how Lizzie or Dizzie would mourn him! Bertie did not share her emotion, but gazed after Alexander with almost approval on his face. Truth to tell, Bertie was just as well pleased Alexander had happened to go casually by at that moment. Bertie had begun to feel the way he had that night —the night before her ladyship had gone a-journeying. As he had been wanting in steadfastness after her going, so now, with her ladyship so near, Bertie had begun to experience, anew, certain definite and pronounced heart palpitations. And might have yielded to the same, and so turned the tables on her ladyship! Her ladyship did not know what a narrow escape she had had!

Bertie, interrupted in this dangerous but fascinating pastime, by Alexander, now pulled himself together. No more Lovers' Lane for him! Honor forbid! And how was he going to tell her ladyship, now, what honor bade him impart? He couldn't; he would go away and write about it. "Good-looking chap, your castaway!" Bertie vouchsafed graciously. "Do you think so?" In a startled voice. "Carries himself as if he had been born to strut around private estates!" laughed Bertie. "It's the clothes," said the lady absent-mindedly. "You dress a hod-carrier in good clothes and he immediately straightens up." "I'd like to talk to the fellow." Patronizingly. "No, no!" Quickly. "Why not?" "I don't think it would be best. You—you see he's very eccentric!" "And is that the reason you give him free run of the place? Frankly, I don't understand it, Estelle."

"Don't try to! Don't assume that managerial tone—yet! One would think the ceremony had already been performed." Bertie turned scarlet and swallowed. The lady noticed and rejoiced. "Why shouldn't I give him free run of the place?" "Why not?" Absently. "And if you begrudge such a little thing—my giving away your clothes, now!—how will it be after?" said the lady. "Will you be preaching economy?" "Glad he's got the clothes," said Bertie hastily. "And if he's short on shirts I'll send down some more—nice silk ones!" "Now you are charming! You see I have a special reason for being nice to him!" "You have?" "Yes; you see, he—he saved my life!" "He did?" "Would you have me consign the savior of my life to the servants' quarters? Would you have me to tell him to eat with the scullery-maids? Would you have me deny him your clothes, your shoes, your shirts?" "No, no!"said Bertie. "Here, give him that!" Handing her his watch. "He has everything else!" "Is this levity?" said the lady severely. "Beg your pardon, but do you mean to say he eats with—not with—" "Me? Yes!" "A porter!" "Exigencies of circumstance! You might have been born a porter!" Bertie disdained this. "How long has he been here?" "Ah, you consider you have the right to—to question me, now!" "Oh, never mind!" Hastily. "But I do mind! And you have the right! He has been here since yesterday." "Yesterday?" "But it's quite all right! He occupied the royal suite, and I—I had Cook for a chaperon, and a very good chaperon she is, too." Bertie gazed at her.

"The royal suite! Whew!" he whistled. "Isn't it romantic?" "Rather!" Looking at her hard. "For him, I mean! As for me—" "For you?"— "My book of romance has been closed!" "Closed?"- Mechanically. "By you!" "By jove, Estelle!" he exclaimed. "Of one thing I'm sure! The man who gets you won't have a dull moment." "Perhaps you flatter yourself!" Bertie blinked. "Here he comes back," he said. The lady thrilled. "You two must meet!" Was Alexander returning to assassinate or to play with his victims? The lady waited expectantly. Strange conduct! He did not look at them as he drew near. Indeed, he seemed oblivious of their presence. Was this but duplicity?

When their backs were turned would he spring upon them? Did he seek to lull them with a sense of false security, and then abruptly, without warning, consummate the dire deed? He got by once more. The lady looked around. Nothing happened. He was reserving his treachery. She came to a sudden resolution. "Alexander!" He stopped. "Come here!" Would he obey? Wonder of wonders, he did. "This is the man," she said to Bertie. "Awh!" said Bertie patronizingly. "Her ladyship tells me you saved her ladyship's life." Alexander did not answer. "A fine fellow! Awh!" "Yes, Alexander's quite uncommon—quite out of the ordinary!" Now would he spring upon them? Alexander's face was like a block of wood— expressionless! "I haven't yet learned the circumstances, my good man," went on the Honorable Bertie, "but you have been greatly privileged, to have saved the life of one of her ladyship's prominence and position!" It was a long speech for the Honorable Bertie and, somehow, he felt it wasn't exactly what he wanted to say, but Bertie was inwardly perturbed and confused. Her ladyship suddenly laughed. She couldn't help it. She was thinking what Bertie would say if only he knew all! The whole dreadful truth! Wouldn't he be an outraged Bertie? Perhaps Alexander would blurt out the terrible secret? Yet he was now oddly silent; strangely still! An impassive, ominous Alexander! Of what was he thinking? Though her life depended on her tact, her ladyship could not restrain her gaiety. "How pompously you said that, Bertie!" she observed. "It was, really, quite unworthy of one usually so clever!" "I get him," said Alexander gravely. "He means he understands your stupid platitudes!"

The look Alexander bestowed upon her again seemed to read her very soul. "What an eye that man has!" thought the lady, but she wasn't going to let herself be intimidated. She looked him in the eye, and for a moment it was a question of what might happen. Alexander's breast, she conceived as a fiery furnace. He had intimated, only too plainly, that he regarded her as his—his goods and chattels! How his gigantic egotism must be boiling! With what delight she could continue to pile on the fuel! Regardless of the outcome! Let a volcano engulf her! She cared not! "Besides," said her ladyship gaily to the Honorable Bertie, "you mustn't enhance, too greatly, the value of his services, or he'll be raising the price!" "The price?" said the Honorable Bertie with a slight frown. "I say, my good fellow—" "There! there!" said her ladyship. "I won't have him scolded." "Oh, I no mind him," said Alexander.

He was standing very straight and steady— meditating what? What crime? He was an inch or so taller than Bertie and even better put-up, although Bertie was an excellent specimen of fine physical manhood. Her ladyship couldn't help making comparisons to Alexander's advantage. Was it right to approve of one's prospective slayer? At least it showed large-mindedness, her ladyship reflected. Bertie found himself shaking his head. "Still, you know, my good fellow, you must really leave it to her ladyship, or"—remembering how impractical her ladyship was about money matters —"to her ladyship's friends!" "Maybe I not get anything," said Alexander shrewdly, "if I leave it to them! Maybe they try to cut it down!" "Maybe they'll do no such thing!" said her ladyship. "Maybe they'll not interfere!" "But—" Bertie eyed Alexander. Dolt! Did he not know he was playing with thunder and lightning?

Her ladyship moved between them. She had seen a spark in Alexander's eye and she divined forces, elemental, about to burst their bonds! "Is my life of so little consequence that we stand here and quibble about the price I am to pay to this gallant"—nothing like flattery to smooth things out!—"gentleman?" "Gentleman?" queried Bertie. The lady threw back her head. "Well, he knew what knives and forks to use," she said. "He never made a mistake, once. If you don't believe me, ask Pelton!" Bertie pondered. "How many courses were there? One?" She regarded the speaker with scorn. "It was a dinner of even larger proportions than usual! Is it likely I would bestow upon the savior of my life an abbreviated repast?" "Is it likely a common porter would eat a large dinner without making a mistake?" "He isn't a common porter. He's an uncommon! Didn't he win a pound from me at billiards, afterward?" "Making hay while the sun shines, eh?"

Alexander held himself aloof but the lady noticed his deep, penetrating eyes were bent very fixedly and inquiringly upon

Bertie, as though seeking to read him up and down and across both ways. There was a burning concentration in Alexander's gaze now. "Got a pound out of you, did he?" said Bertie. "I suppose, under the circumstances, it's up to me to get it back!" As he spoke Bertie grinned. Regular billiard shark, was Bertie! "Good!" said her ladyship, retaliation in her tones. Alexander had played her a trick; it was only right he should be made to suffer. "But perhaps he won't play?" "I play, all right," said Alexander. "How lovely!" said her ladyship. Instead of an assassination they were going to play games.

Of course, the tragedy would be merely postponed. Alexander's manner did not deceive her. She divined the terrible restraint he was imposing upon himself. But "sufficient unto," etc. She led the way to the house gaily. Upon the balcony they encountered the most recent of her ladyship's staff of employees. "This is Miss Handsaw," said her ladyship to Bertie. The Honorable Bertie bestowed upon Miss Handsaw a sour look. "My chaperon!" said her ladyship. "Concession to 'igh respectability and English morality! A very respectable person!" "Looks it!" muttered Bertie, but not loud enough for Miss Handsaw to hear. Then they all entered the house.

Chapter XX
Alexander on his Meddle

"Now for the trimming of Alexander!" thought her ladyship, and settled herself blithely in an easy chair in the billiard-room. Bertie chalked his cue and looked along it with the eye of an expert. Alexander didn't bother taking any such precautions. Then Bertie began and it was charming to watch him; ease, grace and certainty characterized his every play. He made a nice run which her ladyship applauded, while mentally she saw Alexander reluctantly handing over the pound. Cupidity should be punished. Alexander played very poorly at first, and the lady beamed with satisfaction. Then he picked up a bit; then a bit more! Now it was neck and neck.

Then, by a seeming fluke, Alexander won. He put out his hand; Bertie paid. "A bally accident!" he said between his teeth. "Make it two this time. Double or quits!" Alexander eyed the coins wistfully. Cupidity struggled with caution in his gaze. "Afraid?" said the lady derisively. Alexander looked at her. "I'll play."Again it was very close, and again Alexander just.managed to pull off the game in his favor, but he had to struggle mightily; he took so much time over the shots that Bertie waxed sarcastic, and even her ladyship could not refrain from a cutting word or two. Bertie gritted his teeth. "Double or quits!"he said. Alexander looked at the four gold pieces. Caution seemed to get the better of cupidity. "Four birds in the hand," he murmured, "are better—" "Coward!" breathed her ladyship. "And to think my life was saved by such a hero!"

That settled Alexander. "All right! But this is the last!" This time he played more carefully than ever, and again her ladyship "rooted" for Bertie, seeming to forget that Alexander was her savior. His methods were most exasperating; he would start to do something, and then he would do something else, after a period of protracted consideration. "Lightning artist!" grunted Bertie. "Ought to have a time limit!" Alexander won. "Put me to sleep!" muttered Bertie savagely. "That's what he did!" Then he helped himself to the Scotch-and-soda Pelton had brought. "Double or quits!" he said. "If you win, I'm done! All the coin I've got with me! But we have to have a time limit." "No dawdling this time!" From her ladyship. "Eight birds in the hand!" said Alexander, looking at the gold. "Eight gold birds! Why I take chances?" "But suppose there were sixteen?"

That was too much for Alexander. "All right!" "And no dawdling!" repeated her ladyship. "If you dawdle the wager's off, and I shall be the judge." "I'll not dawdle," said Alexander. And he didn't. He hardly looked at the balls; he leaped on them. And the way they flew around and performed made Bertie's eyes bulge. Now Alexander fairly sprinted; he was like a panther on the trail, and brought the game to a close in record time. Bertie stood drooping. "Stung!" he murmured. "Did I dawdle?" said Alexander to the lady. "He's got my clothes, and now he's got my purse," said Bertie. Alexander looked at the money. "Sixteen golden birds in the hand!" "A whole aviary!" snapped Bertie. "Is there anything else I've got you want?" "Maybe," said Alexander, and as he spoke his dark impelling eyes swept to the lady.

"Be thankful you are alive, Bertie!" murmured the latter. Alexander's eyes suddenly snapped. The lady saw. "Yes; I suppose I ought to be glad he hasn't taken my life!" grumbled Bertie. "There is yet time for that," said the lady gaily. Did Alexander smile? She was not sure. "Haven't even got car-fare to get back to London with!" muttered Bertie. "Perhaps you won't need car-fare," said the lady. This time she was sure she saw Alexander smile. "I'll borrow a quid or two from Pelton," said Bertie. "Instead of giving him the customary?" "Oh, you'll all be borrowing if your hero hangs around here much longer," said Bertie in a nasty tone. Alexander continued to look at the coins. "I play you, for your note!"

"No, you don't!" Bertie thrust his hands into his empty pockets. "I put in my dress-suit, the shirts, and the sixteen gold birds, against your note for twenty- five!" "Your dress-suit!" cried Bertie. "I add my shiny shoes!" "Your —" But words failed Bertie. "You won't?" said Alexander with a sweet smile. "I won't!" "You 'fraid?" "I am!" "You call me coward?" said Alexander to the lady. "Me!" He tapped his chest.. "I add silk socks—my pipe—" Bertie took another drink. His hand shook, so great was his agitation. "Perhaps I'd better be crawling away," he said weakly. "Would you leave me?" she said reproachfully. And her eyes added: "Alone with him!"

"But if he should get hold of Pelton first, I shouldn't be able to borrow the car-fare," said Bertie. "Would you not walk back for my sake if you had to, Bertie?" she asked tenderly. Alexander suddenly became very attentive. "I—I—oh, of course," said Bertie huskily. To the lady's fascinated gaze, Alexander's shoulders and arms seemed to become more bulgy and muscular. And what did that sudden tightening of his lips portend? "Maybe you won't be able to walk!" This was playing with fire. She was glad of a chance to change the conversation. "Oh, look who's coming!" she said suddenly, gazing out of the window. "The bishop, and the curate, and their wives, and a few other ladies!" said Bertie blankly. "They've heard I've come back and have called to congratulate me!" "What are you going to do with him?" observed Bertie, jerking his finger toward Alexander. "Introduce him as your guest?"

"Why not?" Vivaciously. "Isn't he? Fortunately, he has a foreign name, and one overlooks a good deal in a foreigner. Little crudities of conversation, for example!" "Oh, I can just hear his light and merry persiflage!" said Bertie with a guffaw. "And I bet he'll hit the bishop for a fiver the first thing. Or preempt his gaiters!" Alexander listened patiently. His was the aspect of a man who was biding his time. Her ladyship skated on thin ice; she knew it, but what matter? "Come," she said in her ordinary society tone, and they went. Nothing especially out of the ordinary happened. Alexander kept an eye on Bertie and did about what he did. The lady had been surprised when Alexander had acquired proficiency in tableware prestidigitation. Now she was doubly surprised when she saw how he picked up drawing room manners by watching Bertie.

He didn't fall over the ladies' feet nor step on their toes. He didn't spill tea down any one's neck or drop his bread-and-butter on the floor, butter-side down, and pick it up again and eat it. In a word, he committed no faux pas. Instead, he seemed quite popular. The gushers, old and young alike, were attracted by his stunning masculine beauty. He talked, too. Or at least he seemed to be moving his lips when her ladyship looked his way. Her ladyship did not have time to observe very particularly; she, herself, was kept rather busy dealing in vague generalities concerning her recent experiences. Incidentally, she imparted very little real information. But what about Alexander in this respect? How much was he telling? Of course, the world would have to know, sometime, what now she was keeping secret, but she wanted to talk things over with her uncle, the lord high chancellor, first! She wanted to be advised what to do about Alexander, or with him, and who could advise better than a lord high chancellor? With his stupendous accumulated wisdom and knowledge! She wondered what would Alexander do, coping with a lord high chancellor? How his assurance would fall from him! What a mere pygmy he would seem, intellectually, in comparison! How he would shrink and shrivel! How small become! How insignificant! Poor Alexander! There was a period of reckoning. Little did he know what was in store for him!

Her ladyship had laid all her plans. She had found time to send a little telegram that would bring results soon. Of course, after the lord high chancellor had blasted Alexander with all the power of his judicial might and reduced him to mere nothingness, her ladyship would plead for him. And—well, then, she would be rather nice to him! All this passed through her mind while chatting gaily, and telling all (nothing!) about her recent experiences. But her ladyship could tell nothing with greater charm than most people can tell a great deal.

She possessed the art of making her nothings pass for a great deal, while most people's great deal passes for nothing. It wasn't necessary to remember what her ladyship said; in fact, it was rather impossible. As well try to put sunbeams or rainbows in cold storage! You can't can the diaphanous, or preserve such airy effervescence in mental fruit jars for future reference. Guests come; guests go. "What a singularly intelligent man Mr."— mentioning Alexander—"is," said the bishop's lady before departing. "Do you find him so?" said her ladyship, in a funny tone. "So well-versed in theology!" Enthusiastically. Now the good woman liked to talk theology. "We agree perfectly," said the bishop's wife. "I suppose," thought her ladyship, "Alexander nodded his head, not knowing what else to do!" But what she said was: "Oh, yes; he's a wonderful authority!"

"I wish he'd come over some time and talk to the bishop!" "I am sure he would be delighted," said the lady, with another funny look. Fancy Alexander taking a dish of tea with the bishop and talking theology! "What a delightful man, Mr."—mentioning Alexander—"is," said a lady who had been called upon to sing a ballad. "He just knows everything about music!" "Everything?" said her ladyship, with another funny look. "Well, almost everything! For example, we agree perfectly on tonal effects." "I'm sure you would do very well singing duets," said her ladyship. "Oh, will you lend him to me?" Enthusiastically. "Reluctantly! For the sake of art!" Think of Alexander singing half a duet! "Art!" murmured a third. "My dear Lady Langlenshire, I congratulate you on your charming guest. One seldom meets a man so well posted. Post-impressionism and all that! We were quite one, in thinking—" They all went, at last. Her ladyship looked at Alexander. "You were quite eclipsed, Bertie!" Bertie looked sulky. "Bally lot of gushers!" he said. "Oh, no! Just ordinary people! But don't feel badly. He almost eclipsed me." Bertie eyed Alexander with supreme disfavor. "I wonder," said the lady, "if he will eclipse the lord high chancellor?" "Bally nerve, I call it!" said Bertie ill-humoredly. "Oh, no," said her ladyship. "It only proves an old proverb." "What's that?" "Silence is golden."

"But pride sometimes has a fall," said the lady, thinking of the lord high chancellor. "I don't fall down," said Alexander confidently. "No?" purred the lady sweetly. "No," said Alexander, drawing himself up like a conqueror and eying Bertie. "When I want something"—looking at her ladyship—"I sweep it"—looking at Bertie—"aside!" "Isn't he delicious?" purred the lady. "'Something!' 'It!' Neuter gender!" "I don't know what the bally deuce he's talking about," said Bertie. "We are slightly at cross-purposes, that is all. He was thinking of 'something' and 'it,' and I was thinking of something else! But what right have we to think? Three people have vouched for his super-cleverness. Connoisseur, judge, arbiter- elegantarium!" "Dick Turpin, or Jesse James, I should call him," said Bertie. "A master of music, art, theology!" mused the lady. "No one ever told me you knew everything, Bertie!" "Did they say that about him?" "Three people! All authorities in their respective lines!" Alexander drew himself up. "I show them," he said proudly. "I suppose," said the lady, "you think you know more than they do?" "Sure," said Alexander. "Only I no tell them that." Shrewdly. "What frightful artfulness!" said the lady. "I know of but one person in the world wise enough to cope with him." "The lord high chancellor has come, your lady-ship," said Pelton, at that moment entering the room. "How apropos!" cried her ladyship. "You will entertain him, Bertie?" Indicating Alexander. "I have matters to discuss with my uncle." "Well, he's got my shirt, my pipe, my boots, my clothes and my money," said Bertie, eying Alexander. "Yes; I think I can entertain him now with tolerable safety." "I'm sure of it!" gurgled the lady, and floated out of the room. For a moment the two men eyed each other. "Have a cigarette," said Bertie ironically, tendering his case. "Thanks!" said Alexander, and took one. Then he looked at the case Bertie had, inadvertently, handed to him. "Nice case!" "Eh?" Bertie started. Alexander made as if to hand it back, but his gaze was wistful. "Keep it," said Bertie. "You got everything else! Forgot I had this! I apologize!"

"That's all right!" Complacently. "Maybe I get a better one some time! This all right for now!" "You take such a load from my mind," said Bertie. "So glad you may find it of service temporarily!" "Have a match!" said Alexander. And handed Bertie one. "Thanks!" said Bertie. "Thanks so much!" "Eh? It go out? Have another!" Bertie took it. "Don't overwhelm me," he said. "You think you marry her?" said Alexander nonchalantly, nodding toward the door through which her ladyship had passed. Bertie turned red. "None of your d—" He checked himself. "What business is it of yours?" "H'um!" Alexander didn't commit himself but studied Bertie. "You no want to talk about her?" Shrewdly. "I certainly don't!" snapped Bertie. He was about to add, with a sneer: "With a porter, even if he is privileged!"

But he didn't! Bertie had reasons for not wanting to quarrel about her ladyship or to pose as her champion. "Very fine woman!" said Alexander, his glance like an eagle's, bent on Bertie. "That's neither here nor there," said Bertie curtly. Did the fellow wish to force him into that champion- role? "You think so?" pursued Alexander with burning gaze. "I don't think!" "I see! I have eyes," continued Alexander. "Out there!" He meant in Lovers' Lane. Bertie, enraged, felt himself getting deeper in the toils. But how could he give way to that overwhelming anger? He had been indiscreet. "What she tell you, eh?" said Alexander. Bertie wanted to strangle him but refrained. "Can't we find some more interesting topic of conversation?" he observed desperately. "No, no; I don't mean that! Her ladyship is always interesting, of course! More—more profitable topic, was probably what I meant to say!" "Profitable?" said Alexander. "You mean you play billiards?" "Anything!" With a groan. "My dress-suit, the shiny shoes, the sixteen gold birds, against your note for twenty-five?"

"Anything," repeated Bertie, and followed Alexander.

Her ladyship greeted her uncle affectionately. "When did you arrive, my dear? Yesterday! And didn't let me know until to-day?" "Well, you see, I wanted time to recover myself." "Yes? You have, no doubt, experienced many vicissitudes. We have worried about you. But where did you land? Folkstone?" "No; on the beach, below!" "Bless my soul! How?"

Her ladyship unfolded the entire story. The lord high chancellor listened without comment. "And now, what do you think of it?" said the lady, when at last she had concluded. "Bless my soul!" said the lord high chancellor. "Is that all?" "All,"he answered. "But your high legal acumen—your judicial wisdom—what of them?" cried the lady indignantly. "Don't you see, you've got to tell me what to do next!" "I?" said the lord high chancellor with a start. "Of course! Aren't you the wisest man in England? At least, everyone says so! And haven't I been depending on you? You are to tell me what to do!" "I?" repeated the chancellor again. "Is that all you have to say?" "Bless my soul!" "Is that all?" "God bless my soul!" The lady waved her hands despairingly. "And I looked to you!" she said reproachfully.

"I am afraid you overestimate my poor talents, my dear child," said the chancellor humbly. "Only a brain that involved you in such a quagmire could extract you therefrom!" "You mean you desert me?" "On the contrary! In nautical phraseology, I feel it my duty to stand by." "That's all right, then," said her ladyship in livelier accents. "When people talk about high respectability, or duty, I feel safer. Now, I am positive it will come out all right!" "And I, my dear child"—in the same humble tones—"would sooner trust your intuition than my wisdom." "Is that what you call 'standing by'? It sounds to me more like evasion," said the lady. "Watchful waiting, my dear," corrected the lord high chancellor. "Wisdom waiting on intuition!" "Wisdom shouldn't wait. I want to be guided by your wisdom." "Oh, no, you don't, my dear child," said the great man.

She stiffened. "You only think you do," he added. "You give me credit, then, for not knowing my own mind?" "A charming attribute!" "Mental weakness!" she scoffed. "Mental grace! As there are two sides to every question, a certain uncertainty is both gracious and human. When you plunged wildly into this adventure you were not guided by wisdom. Since wisdom had no part in the enterprise, why thrust wisdom into it at this late day?" "Instead of standing by, this now looks more like throwing me overboard," said the lady indignantly. "And I thought you would settle it all in a second!" "Oh, no; you didn't!" "I beg your pardon." "You only thought you thought! This matter is not one to be settled in a second. It may take years." "Years!" said her ladyship blankly. "I don't understand. Of course, there is only one thing to do." "You mean to hale him into the courts and toss him out of the window, neck and breeches? Good! Now we are getting practical, at last." "But," said the lady, "I don't want him tossed out!" "How then?" "Could you not accomplish the same result more—decorously?" "Fudge! A common porter!" "An uncommon one!" said the lady. "He has certain unusual traits." "So I gathered when you were telling me the story!" "Let us be just! It was I who asked him to marry me!" "And he did—for a consideration? Ahem!" "But didn't he nearly lose his life on my account? And didn't he save mine? And bring me ashore like—like Neptune bearing Aphrodite?"

"So you have informed me before!" Dryly. "I could only think of some fabulous watergod!" "A common porter; a water-god!" "But he isn't a common—" "More repeating." "He keeps getting less and less common all the time! He has a marvelous gift of mimicry. He learned what knives and forks to use almost at once by watching me, and what to do in a drawing-room by watching Bertie. He has become a marvel of grace; he even overshadows me." "Dear me!" "In the conversational art, though, he only says:'Yes' and 'No'!" "Ha!" said the lord high chancellor. "He is terribly artful. He deceives people. He makes them think he is gifted with wonderful knowledge by just sitting still and looking wise." "A good many of us do that," said her uncle. "I have myself, on occasions, resorted to the subterfuge."

"You?" "I!" "Well, at any rate, people go away singing his praises. And that isn't the worst! He has a frightful cupidity. He has all Bertie's clothes, and his pipe, and his money, and, I am not sure, he is not planning to take his life." "Bless my soul!" said the lord high chancellor. "In fact, he may, already, have taken it!" "God bless—" "And he made love to the cook because she was a three-hundred pounder, and frightened her so she went scooting down the highway." "Bless my—" "I think she's going yet! And because he liked them that way"—breathlessly—"I was forced to engage a different kind of a chaperon." "Different kind!" "Like a 'atchet, or a bean-pole!" The chancellor made a sound. "And all this happening in a highly respectable community!"

"A good deal might happen in any community, my dear, where you are!" said the lord high chancellor. "But you spoke of Bertie Brindleton? Is that honorable young gentleman here?" "He is!" "Then you've heard about his marriage—" "His what? —Oh, yes!" In light fluty tones. "Bertie was telling me all about it! Whom did he marry?" Again the chancellor stared. "Tossie Tiddles! Gayety girl! She got him in her toils shortly after you left!" "Of course! Though that isn't exactly the way Bertie put it to me," remarked her ladyship. "Naturally not! I suppose Bertie thinks he got her in his toils?" Her ladyship began to laugh. "Poor Bertie!" And then: "Do me a favor!" "A million!" Gallantly. "Do not let Bertie know I—I am married!" "Why not? You do not seem dreadfully worried about it?"Ironically.

"I? Oh, no! It's Bertie who's worried, and I want him to be!" "I understand perfectly," said the chancellor, not understanding at all. "You see, I want Bertie to leave thinking I am heart-and-fancy free!" "But suppose he elects to remain?" "He can't. He hasn't any clothes. His garments are already occupied. He hasn't even a clean collar." "Bless my— But who?" "Alexander!" "And when am I to have the privilege of gazing on this interesting gentleman?" "Now! And, uncle, you may go as far as you please!" "Divorce?" Her ladyship caught her breath. Then the spirit of the Langlenshires looked out of her eyes. "Why—why, what alternative could there be?"

CHAPTER XXII
WORDS OF WISDOM

"What! In the billiard-room again?" said her ladyship. Bertie put down his cue hastily. "So glad you've come!" "Is it as bad as that?" "He's won a fifty-pound note, and was just proposing to make it a hundred." "Why, Alexander!" said the lady, shaking reprovingly her fair head. "Before that, he got my cigarette case!" "Bless my soul!" said the lord high chancellor, buttoning his frock coat and folding his arms over his pocketbook. "Isn't he wonderful, uncle?" said the lady, indicating Alexander. "I quite agree with you, my child. But won't you present me to this gentleman of so many and diversified accomplishments?"

The lady did, introducing the lord high chancellor by all his titles. The chancellor greeted Alexander with all the grace of the old school, but Alexander did not appear abashed. He was imitating the lord high chancellor's manner now. "Isn't he wonderful?" said the lady again. Here was Alexander, a gentleman of the old school! But the chancellor did not answer. He was regarding Alexander with considerable earnestness and attention. "You will excuse me, please," here Bertie put in hastily. "Got just time to catch my train!" "Must you go?" said the lady, with a trace of emotion. "And when shall I see you again? To-morrow perhaps?" Bertie mentioned something about telegraphing. "Very well," said the lady. "And that little matter—please do not speak of it!"

"I won't," mumbled Bertie. She went with him as far as the door. "In about a week!" she murmured. "What?" said Bertie miserably. "You may tell everyone." "Great!" In a hollow voice. "I wish now I had let you!" she whispered, just outside the door. "Down in Lovers' Lane, you know!" "Got to go!" said Bertie hoarsely. "To-morrow, then, or next day?" She held out her hand. "I'll telegraph," he repeated nervously. "Are you happy?" "In—in the seventh heaven!" lied Bertie, like a gentleman. She thrilled with a happy laugh. "Isn't it wonderful?" "Wonderful!" lied Bertie again. The worst was, she looked so beautiful and tantalizing and altogether alluring, his heart was going thump- thump!

"If only you didn't have to go so soon!" said the lady. "What am I saying?" "Good-by!" whispered Bertie wildly. Heavens! how she loved him! He fled. The lady went back into the billiard-room where Alexander was toying with the balls, and the lord high chancellor was watching him. "Did he offer to play you a match?" said the lady to her uncle. "He did, my dear." "And you declined?" "Regretfully." "Oh, Alexander," breathed the lady, "is there no limit to your propensities to acquire other people's possessions?" "I play fair," said Alexander with a sweet smile. "Granted! But is it a clean-cut sporting proposition?" "I no cheat," said Alexander. "Oh, uncle, you put it to him!" she implored. "If we don't curb Alexander's sporting proclivities, what will become of our guests? Would we not soon find ourselves shunned—isolated by society?" "There is an alternative!" "You no want me to play billiards, eh?" said Alexander. "All right! I won't. I play bridge, instead!" "No, you won't," said the lady quickly. "You'd soon have all the money in the kingdom!" "Can you play bridge?" said the chancellor, studying him. "I learn soon. I learn games mighty easy! I hear it bully good game for country-houses. I do very well!" "I'm sure of it," said the lady. "Is not money good?" said Alexander simply. "What are you going to do with a man like that?" said the lady despairingly to her uncle. "He should do very well in London. His talents are lost down here." "In the city!" said the lady enthusiastically. "He would soon own the Bank of England."

"How would you like to migrate to town, Alexander?" said the lord high chancellor. "To pack your things now and go back with me?" Her ladyship started. "Pack my things!" repeated Alexander. "Or Bertie Brindleton's! Ha, ha! Think what a good joke it would be on Bertie!" But somehow Alexander did not seem to see the joke. "You want to take me away from here?" "I do." "For

good?" "You mean forever?" "Of course!" Her ladyship turned
her head. It was too absurd! Whence this sudden little thrill of
emotion? Engendered by the novelty of the situation, no doubt!
"From her?" went on Alexander. "Of course!" "I don't see her
any more?" "Naturally not!" Alexander pondered. "I go away; I
never come back; I never see her?" he repeated, as if to make sure
that he got it all clearly defined in his brain. "That is a summary
of what I have already informed you," said the chancellor. "You
mean she never come to me?" "Naturally, if you never see her
more!" said the chancellor patiently. "She forget me?" "I trust so!
Proper thing to do!" "You want me to go?" said Alexander to the
lady. "You—you don't think it could be otherwise, do you?" she
answered, but her voice had an artificial inflection. "I never see
you?" "Naturally," she said. "And you never see me?" "Naturally!" Alexander looked at her. "You no speak in your voice. You
speak in his." "Not at all!" said the chancellor hastily. "I am but
'standing by.' The lady is capable of speaking her own mind." "If
those your words," said Alexander to the lady, "you come out
in garden, alone with me, to say them!" A red spot appeared on
the lady's cheek. Heavens! Alexander appeared handsome at that
moment. As he thus challenged her he looked like an aggrieved
Greek god. "No, no," she said. "I—I wouldn't trust myself alone
with him. Not for worlds!" The lord high chancellor looked from
one to the other. "You fear he may do you an injury, my dear?"
"Can you ask? Look at him!" Alexander did not look as fierce as
might have been expected. In fact, his eyes were almost tender;
deeply introspective! "He doesn't look exactly ferocious to me,"
observed the chancellor. "It's—it's his artfulness! He wouldn't let
you see!"

"I won't touch her with a little finger," observed Alexander. "I promise only to use words!" "No, no; it wouldn't do, at
all!" said the lady quickly. "I—I am afraid of him!" Alexander
folded his arms. "I—I ever give you cause to be afraid of me?"
"Well, you're very big!" "A fault of nature, my dear!" interposed

the chancellor justly. "And very strong!" Alexander smiled. There was sadness in his smile. "Did I ever beat you?" "I will confess," said the lady, "you have spared me—so far!" Alexander looked at her. The domineering eyes were soulful; they sent little thrills into her. "I promise to strike you— never!" he said. "Nothing like that! Something—different!" The lady shrank back in her chair. "Say something!" she gasped to the chancellor. The chancellor said something quickly—in some language she did not understand. Alexander, wheeling, responded in the same language. "I thought so," said the lord high chancellor. A whimsical smile swept Alexander's lips. He stood, leaning forward a little, his head slightly down-bent. "What was that you said?" asked the lady. "Let Alexander tell you," said the lord high chancellor, and left the room.

Chapter XXIII
The Beginning of the New

"And now," said the lady, facing Alexander. Alexander, for one so handsome, looked sheepish. 'I'm sorry," he said. "About what?" "He spoke when he did!" "And why should you be sorry?" she demanded. "Because I thought I was beginning to 'get on'!" "Get on? What do you mean?" "With you!" Humbly. "You thought that? You dared think that?" "This porter—" "I dared," he said in a low tone. She didn't quite recognize that tone. It was different— something new!

"Yes, I'm sorry," he repeated, "and yet, I'm glad" "About what?" "That you didn't actually kick me out! Though you would have been justified!" Whence came these finely modulated tones? "You still seem very presuming!" "I wouldn't be," said Alexander. "It is my heart's desire to lay my life's service at your feet." "Say that again!" cried the lady, standing in a daze. "And every service I shall count as a sweetest boon!" What music was this? Alexander's voice had lost all harshness and stridency. His tones were deep and mellifluous. So the surf might murmur on the shore. "I hear," said the lady, as one trying to catch a new song, "but I do not seem to understand." "Do you not see, it is my heart that I am laying at your feet?"

"Your heart?" The lady felt her own move. "What heart? How do I know you have a heart? I seem to have stepped from somewhere, into somewhere else." "Step into my life," said Alexander, in booming tones, "forever! And I will build there a shrine for you!" "Very pretty! Only more inexplicable!" "No more so than sunlight, birds' songs, the joy of life, the ecstasy of another's presence!" "Ecstasy?" "For me!" "A poet?" Staring at him. "Not I! Love speaks." "Love!—a monster!" "Love, a cooing dove!" murmured the big Alexander insidiously. "Love, as gentle as the summer breeze that hardly dares to kiss the rose!" "Eh?" said the lady.

"Love as humble as the brook that washes at the feet of lilies, on the woodland bank!" "Eh?" said the lady once more.

But Alexander was not done. Like Orlando, he seemed to be able to go on forever. "And yet love"—swelling his chest—"as aspiring as the cloud that dares to float before the refulgent and beneficent orb of day!" "Charming!" murmured the lady. "And all the while I was apprehensive you were going to woo me with a club!" "Do you fear to step out into the garden with me now?" "I am quite sure my uncle would not have left me here with you, alone, had he not felt I would be perfectly safe in your company." "Safe?" His eyes glowed. "With me? Why, I would hold you against the world." "Would you? That sounds reassuring." Alexander put out a big hand and just touched the golden hair. His fingers, for all his air of big assurance, were uncertain as if he were caressing the air. "Come!" he said. "Well?"—After all, it was the lord high chancellor's fault. They stepped outdoors.

Miss Handsaw saw them and started to follow —at a discreet distance. Alexander stopped. Her ladyship looked at him, almost timidly. Alexander seemed to have usurped all authority. "You are discharged," he said, frowning at Miss Handsaw. "I takes my orders from her," said Miss Handsaw. "It's quite all right," said her ladyship hastily. "Indeed!" said Miss Handsaw. "Was I 'ired by 'im?" "No; only fired by him!" said Alexander. "Ha, ha!" "Just his playful ways!" said her ladyship hastily. "You are to go. But you will be sent a month's wages." "I'll go," said Miss Handsaw ominously. "And it's not for me to say what people will be saying!" "Tell them," said Alexander, "There are hearts that say: 'Boo!' and likewise: 'Pooh!' to 'igh respectability! Tell them we are free as eagles that soar above mountain-tops!"

"Lor'!" "Is it wise?" said her ladyship musingly. "What?" said Alexander. "Thus to cast all conventions to the winds!" "If you're arsking me?" began Miss Handsaw. "She isn't," said Alexander promptly. Miss Handsaw looked like a hatchet—all edge. "Ha, ha!" laughed her ladyship nervously. "Just his playful—" "Plyeful?" The edges of Miss Handsaw's lips curled. "Tell them we snap our fingers at high respectability," repeated Alexander. "Just like MacDuffy!" murmured her ladyship. "Who says bishops is humbugs!" "That we live our own lives!" went on Alexander. "You might add, however," said her ladyship, "this gentleman is my husband.", "Oh!" said Miss Handsaw, disappointed. "To 'Boo!' and 'Pooh!' I will now add: 'Shoo'!" said Alexander.

And with such a sudden gesture that Miss Handsaw flew! "Oh, oh!" said her ladyship, laughing. "Where am I? Or where are we? And, somehow, I seem to have thrown my cap over the windmill. I don't seem to know any of the whys and where-fors, or to care much!" "That's as it should be," said Alexander, as Miss Handsaw vanished from sight like a startled exclamation point. "Do the leaves question the night-wind that causes them to rustle? Do the leaping waves make inquiry of the moonbeams? Does the nightingale say to the rose:'Why do I sing?'" "Go on,"said the lady. "You are a kind of a magical porter, I suppose—like the one in the Arabian Nights. And you talk like a volume of poetry to preserve the unities—poetic justice, or something like that! I am a little mixed up on these ethical questions." "What do they matter?" said Alexander vigorously. "I am yours; you are mine! What else is there to say? What else possibly could be said?" "Nothing, I suppose," said the lady humbly, falling in with this grand and exalted idea. "Unless one did, or might, confess to a little curiosity?" "Huh!" said Alexander. She tried to bear up beneath his lofty glance. "You mean, what did your uncle say?" "Yes. I could see that he knew you, the way he looked at you from the first! It caused me to wonder. Why should he have known you?" Alexander looked around. Was he seeking to evade her? "It was here I saw you and another —" She waved her hand airily. "Absolutely nothing!" she said. "Only to punish him!" "Punish?" One could see Alexander thought that an odd way to punish— "Yes, I wished to make him suffer!" "For an impertinence?" A little of the old rumbling Alexander!

"For conceit!" "You led him to do that?" Was this fire in his eye? "Because it was the last thing he wanted to do!" her ladyship found herself saying hastily. "Explain!" "Is that a command?" "A petition!" "Oh!" Suspiciously. "A humble petition!" She explained. "Ha, ha!" said Alexander. "A rude and boisterous laugh for a poet!" she observed. "Oh, I'm laughing like a man!" "I had quite a bit of you as a man," said the lady. "Be a poet once more!" Alexander touched her lips with his. So a leaf might have swept by. "Shameless!" said the lady, apostrophizing herself. "And I do not even know who you are!" "Yet you come to me?"

"I?" His arm encircled but hardly touched. "You!" "Madness!" she said. "Also hardly respectable!" He gathered her to him. "Shocking!" said the lady. But her breath came fast, and so the poet really kissed the lady. "And now," said the lady breathlessly, "Who are you?" "Your lover." "Who else?" "Your husband." "Who else?" "You called me a—a water-imp once!" "Imp?" she said scornfully. "But never mind!" "Maybe it was Neptune?" "That's all very well, as far as it goes," said the lady. "But it doesn't go very far. And don't you think I've been rather patient to permit you to proceed thus far without—"

"Must we disturb the dream?" murmured Alexander. "Would you force me to go to my uncle and say: 'Who is this man who has—has grabbed my heart, and is squeezing the same in his big fist?'" "Do you think that adequately expresses—" he began with large indignation. "How would you put it?" "Who is this man—" began Alexander. "This man"—looking at her—"who has cast his—his whole heart at the earth at my feet?" "Can it be?" she asked. "You—you who laughed—and jested and smiled—and seemed so —well, so utterly oblivious to the torturing flames of love?" Was she laughing? Alexander's eyes flamed. "There are flames within the earth, even beneath the snows," he said. "Cold flint has sparks, yet you must strike it right to find them." "What's that to do with who you are?" she countered.

"What matters the worldly tabulation?" he rumbled. "It

helps," said the lady. "For example, if you got lost, it would help to find you." Alexander glowed. Response courteous? The lady's answer was saccharine. He swam in honey. "That's so," he said. There was a reason why people should be tabulated with names and labeled with addresses like merchandise. A good reason! So if they got lost— He had never thought of that before. Clever! He devoured her with his eyes. Likewise he touched her hand tenderly to his lips. The lady half-closed her eyes; for the moment she forgot curiosity. Idly drifting! What could be pleasanter? A dream for a day! Or a few minutes! A leaf fell to her lap as she sat on the marble bench; she took it in her fingers and touched her lips with it. Even nature seemed sympathetic. Alexander took the leaf and pressed his lips where hers had touched it. Then he put it in his pocket—left side!

"A solicitous little leaf!" said the lady. "It got its reward!" said Alexander. He put her head against his broad shoulder and she let it stay there. A little animal peeked at them; found nothing interesting in the spectacle and went back to its tree. Alexander breathed deeply; likewise, he gazed at the heavens. His broad chest rocked—a cradle for the golden head! Light laughter awoke him. He started. He was conscious he was holding said head on its resting-place. "Am I—making myself ridiculous?" he inquired. "Not at all!" said the lady. "It is all eminently satisfying, only, unfortunately, I have a sense of humor." "Humor!" "Pray forgive! And don't think me unfeeling. I couldn't help laughing." "At such a moment," said Alexander, "a moment divine, you experience only—merriment?" "Oh, no! And that is why I laughed, I suspect. I felt myself being wafted away—to realms ineffable! I don't know where. Perhaps you can enlighten me?" "You jest?" The reproach in Alexander's tones was prodigious. "You—cold as ice!" "No, no! It was just that! I was floating— floating—and I just caught myself in time!" The red lips smiled. "Or rather, that sense of humor caught me!" "And what did it say to you?" "It said: 'Whose shoulder is this?'" "Ha, ha!" "You see the joke?" He took her head in his hands. "Ha, ha! That is funny!"He looked deep into her eyes—laughing eyes! "Love laughs!" he said. "Why shouldn't it? Isn't love happy? "'Whose shoulder?'" "Well, whose?" Alexander gazed at her tenderly. "How beautiful you are!" "Is that an evasion?"

"Eh?" "Never mind." she said. "What does it matter? Don't tell me! I'm sure it must be quite ail right and 'ighly respectable and all that, or my uncle would not have turned me over to your tender mercies. But he did take you off your guard, didn't he, when he spoke to you in that language so foreign to my ears?" "He did," said Alexander. "What did he say?" "He said:'I am glad to. meet you again, Prince Milanof!'" said Alexander sheepishly. "Oh, that's it," said the lady quietly. "I'm sorry," said Alexander humbly. "Will that help?" she said more quietly. "Will that bring back my porter?" "I'm sorry," he repeated more contritely. "But that doesn't do any good. It—it doesn't restore anything." "I know," he said. Alexander looked unhappy. "You might as well explain," said the lady resignedly.

Alexander sighed. "The porter—the man — wanted to win you," he said. "I had so much of this prince business. I wanted to forget it." "Why?" "I was a follower of Tolstoi and I suspect I made myself what you English would call a bally nuisance to my government. But I detested autocratic power. At any rate, I was given my choice between fleeing, and a long, enforced vacation, eastward! I had met your uncle on one or two occasions at the court of Petrograd. He remembered me. As porter, I have since been enabled to serve my government. You can imagine how? I passed as a Greek. Indeed, I am free to return to my own country now at any time. A portion of my estates have, I believe, been restored. I can go back. But I only want to—as one of the people! The old order is going—so fast—crumbling! Why could they not see?—The new—the people, for the people."He paused. For the moment his vision was bent afar. She, too, was still. Something held her silent. Then near them a bird began to sing and

Alexander stirred. His eyes returned to hers. Somehow, the lady felt a different nearness—a larger nearness?—She couldn't define the feeling. "Listen!" The birds! "Fussing in a bush!" laughed the lady. "Well, I have lost my porter. And in his place a poet has foisted himself upon me. I suppose I have no choice but to accept the responsibility!" "Sadly?" he said. Her answer was 'ighly unrespectable. "Gladly!" her lips said on his. The lord high chancellor watched them return. "All right?" he said. "Quite," said the lady. "Fine," said Alexander. "I thought I could trust him to you—I mean, you to him, my dear," observed the lord high chancellor. "The prince is an idealist; you are eminently practical. It should prove an ideal match." "I trust I shall prove worthy of her," said Alexander humbly. "I feel my own limitations fearfully," said the lady. "Do you?" said the chancellor in an odd tone. "How about that, Alexander?" "Does one ask the sweetest perfume to be sweeter? Does one say to the sunlight, 'Why aren't you brighter?'" Alexander frowned. "As well criticize the music of the spheres!" "Should I keep him, or not, uncle?" "Since you ask my advice, after having already concluded what to do, I will state, in my humble opinion, you could not do better." "Poor Bertie!" said the lady. "I must send him a telegram." "A telegram?" said the chancellor. "I don't want him to feel bad any longer. I don't want any one to feel bad."

Alexander said nothing. "Dinner," said Pelton, looking in at that moment "And Alexander not yet dressed in the Honorable Bertie's beautiful evening togs!" said the lady. "Never mind!" And then, as they went in: "Don't pretend!" "What?" asked Alexander. "That you don't know without watching me what knives and forks to eat with! Which reminds me: What will the servants say?" "The servants?" said the lord high chancellor. "Yes! You see, they appointed themselves my guardians, and the guardians of high English respectability. Very nice of them!" "Most commendable!" said the chancellor. "But now, uncle, to relieve their apprehensions, you must explain." "Gladly! Explaining is one of the great-

est privileges of my high office." "Since Alexander 'shooed' poor
Miss Handsaw away, they'll be worrying worse than ever."

"That won't do. Call them in after dinner, Pelton. The expla-
nation, my dear, will be masterly." And it was! One or tw'o of
the maids almost wept as his lordship chopped off the Finger of
Scorn and replaced it with the uplifted Hands of Approval. He
smashed the withering blight of doubt and planted a flower in
its place. He set said flower in a beautiful garden. Morality was
like a modest English garden; no tiger-lilies wanted there! "Nor
'uman-tigers!" From Pelton, sotto voce. He eulogized the Committee promulgated for the Uplift of Master and Mistress, and
recommended a national organization along these lines, in the
event of the creation of which her ladyship would be glad to be
a patroness, and he, to serve as a patron. "I, too," said Alexander
modestly. "You hear the prince?" said the chancellor. "'Er ladyship's 'usband!" From Jane proudly.

"As I've made you extra work," said her ladyship, "you should
have extra pay. I'm sure I should pay for having my morals properly guarded!" "But, your ladyship," stammered Jane, "there wasn't
no real need!" "But there might have been! The fact there was not
a real need, and never may be, makes the need of the committee
the more imperative. Am I not right?" To the chancellor. "Absolutely!" Rubbing his nose. "It is to guard against contingencies!"
"Ten pounds apiece for you from me!" said Alexander. "And 'im
a-wearin' of the Honorable Bertie's clothes!" whispered Pelton to
Jane. And then aloud: "Begging your pardon, your 'ighness, but
'ow about MacDuffy? Does that include 'im?" "As you have to
drop an 'h' from 'highness,' Pelton, I would suggest that hence-
forth you address me as 'Sir." "But——" Dismayed.

"You see, I dropped the 'prince,' myself, some time ago."
"For why?" said the horrified Pelton. "Bally nuisance!" "Then
her ladyship ayn't a princess?" murmured the disappointed Jane.
"Don't look so downhearted," spoke up her ladyship. "You see,
there are to be no more grand dukes or princes, in Russia. So the

prince dropped the title—" "Before it dropped him," said Alexander. "And most of my estates! Gone, quite properly, too—for cabbage-patches. For one feudal lord, we are to have a thousand Mrs. Wiggses." "A very common person," said Jane, with a toss of the head. "From h'America!" "And Russia!" said Alexander. "The Russia of the future! We shall not only have our Mrs. Wiggses, but Mr. Wiggses, too!" "Thank 'Eaven, this is h'England!" said Pelton. "Where we still 'ave our clawsses and our h'acres—"

"How can I break it to him?" murmured her ladyship. "The truth is, Pelton, I am going to dispose of my superfluous acres— the idle ones, you know—" "Your ladyship means to sell—" "No. Give—renounce— restore —I am not sure of the proper word— " Turning to the lord high chancellor. "Don't ask me," said that individual weakly. Pelton forgot himself. "Great 'Eavens! h'England will be populated by little Wiggses." "Zee Voltadan idea!" chirped Jacques. "Zee every man with zee every cabbage-patch! Mon Dieu! Zee Mr. Wiggs—he be zee Englishman of zee future—and zee Mrs. Wiggs—she represent zee lovely Mrs. John Bull." Pelton breathed hard. "Shall you be a-wanting of us, at all? H'after?—" It wasn't a chaperon her ladyship needed; it was a keeper. Only Alexander's eyes shone with a vast approval. "Oh, yes. I expect to maintain an establishment. One mustn't become a public-charge, you know." Pelton groaned. "It h'all comes of your ladyship cornin' 'ome, like that!" "Unconventionally?" "With one shoe h'on and the other shoe h'off, limpin' from h'anywhere—" "f -followed by 'im!" said the confused Jane. "A prince w'ot ayn't a prince!" half-bitterly from Pelton. "That will do, Pelton. And you may all go. Thank you so much." "Much!" said the lord high chancellor. "Much!" said Alexander. "Wishing your ladyship every 'appiness!" murmured Pelton. "Hear! Hear!" said Tommy. The others murmured in like vein—then vanished. "And now," said the lord high chancellor, simulating an endeavor to conceal a yawn, "Have I, likewise, your permission to retire, my dear?"

"But, my dear uncle, we've hardly had time yet to get acquainted, all over again." "Indeed?" Dryly. "For me, the day has seemed a rather full occasion. Besides, don't you think I deserve a little rest after my oratorical efforts?" "Go, then!" she said. And he went.

The lady and Alexander seated themselves in a corner of the great, dimly-lighted hall. "Who is this MacDuffy, Pelton spoke of?" asked Alexander. Her ladyship explained—how MacDuffy wouldn't have anything to do with guarding her morals. "Ha! I must reward him!" said Alexander. "Handsomely!" "Do you wish my advice?" "I implore it." Think of talking together about domestic affairs like that! Alexander settled back with a wondrous sense of domestic felicity.

"I think," said the lady, "you have a misconception of the situation." "You should know," said Alexander. Words which fell from such softly-curving lips should be respected—nay, reverenced! "MacDuffy did not refrain from joining the committee because of confidence in any supernatural discretion on my part. He was indifferent. He didn't care. I might have gone to the D. bow-wows, for all of him." "D. bow-wows," said Alexander, puzzled. "Same as throwing your cap over the windmill," explained the lady. "If he didn't care," said Alexander, with a frown, "why should I reward him?" "Why? Besides, think of the demoralizing effect it would have on the others!" "Others?" "Servants!" "Demoralizing?—oh, of course! It would be apt to demoralize them, wouldn't it?" said Alexander, with a funny look.

"Frightfully! One has to be careful. They might all up and leave us." "Us!" Alexander gazed at her. Blissful plural! "Shall I light your cigarette?" said the lady. "No. Nothing extraneous!" "Extraneous?" Lifting her brow. "Only you!" The lady's eyes were very bright. "Are you glad you didn't turn me from the door?" he laughed. "Don't ask me what I'm glad about." "Ah!" Triumphantly. "What did I tell you? Love doesn't reason." "It certainly does not," said the lady. "When one feels like ceasing to think, or to have logical sequences of thought— What does it portend? Brain-storm?" "Heart-storm!" said Alexander. But it was a very gentle tempest that burst upon her.

THE END

Suggested Reading

Cather, Willa. *O Pioneers!* N.p.: Dover Thrift Editions, 1913. Print. Unabridged.

Faulkner, William. *The Sound and the Fury*. N.p.: Vintage International, 1929. Print. The Corrected Text.

Fitzgerald, F. Scott. *This Side of Paradise*. N.p.: Charles Scribner's Sons, 1920. Print.

Isham, Frederic S. *Under the Rose*. 1st ed. Indianapolis: Bobbs Merrill Company, 1903.

Isham, Frederic S. *Half a Chance*. 1st ed. Indianapolis: Bobbs Merrill Company, 1909.

Isham, Frederic S. *The Nutcracker*. 1st ed. Indianapolis: Bobbs Merrill Company.

Isham, Frederic S. *The Social Bucaneer*. 1st ed. Indianapolis: Bobbs Merrill Company, 1910.

Isham, Frederic S. *Lady of the Mount*. 1st ed. Indianapolis: Bobbs Merrill Company, 1908.

James, Henry. *The Turn of the Screw*. New York City: Macmillan Publishers, 1898. Print.

Wharton, Edith. *Ethan Frome*. N.p.: Charles Scribner's Sons, 1911. Print.

www.ingramcontent.com/pod-product-compliance
Lightning Source LLC
Chambersburg PA
CBHW021921170626
46807CB00007B/2928